PENGUIN BOOKS

A TEMPORARY AFFAIR

'Like a perfect soufflé, *A Temporary Affair* is light but satisfying, beautifully executed and delicious in its beguiling simplicity' – *Sunday Independent*

'Chic and larky' – *SHE*

'A wonderfully crafted romantic thriller that enchants and intrigues until the very last breath' – *Irish Times*

'Bags of style and tension' – *Company*

'Great fun, and – best of all – the first in a series featuring Sophie Fitt' – *Image*

'Insouciant, scattered and witty, Sophie is a promising fictional creation and could rank up there beside Anna Lee in no time at all … a very stylish début indeed'
– *Sunday Press*

G000147136

ABOUT THE AUTHOR

Imogen Parker was born in 1958 in Hertfordshire. She has lived in Rome, New York and Madrid and has had a number of jobs – as an au pair, box-office manager, shop assistant, secretary and literary agent. As well as writing, she now works in television. She lives in London with her husband.

Her second Sophie Fitt novel, *Something Funny*, has recently been published by Hamish Hamilton.

A TEMPORARY AFFAIR

Imogen Parker

PENGUIN BOOKS

PENGUIN BOOKS

Published by the Penguin Group
Penguin Books Ltd, 27 Wrights Lane, London W8 5TZ, England
Penguin Books USA Inc., 375 Hudson Street, New York, New York 10014, USA
Penguin Books Australia Ltd, Ringwood, Victoria, Australia
Penguin Books Canada Ltd, 10 Alcorn Avenue, Toronto, Ontario, Canada M4V 3B2
Penguin Books (NZ) Ltd, 182–190 Wairau Road, Auckland 10, New Zealand

Penguin Books Ltd, Registered Offices: Harmondsworth, Middlesex, England

First published by Hamish Hamilton 1994
Published in Penguin Books 1995
1 3 5 7 9 10 8 6 4 2

For
John Parker

I

If I had taken my mother's advice, I would have spent the summer doing a typing course. As it was, I wandered around Edinburgh, dressed in an opaque, red bodysuit and sandwich boards. By the time our revue opened, I had a cold and severe laryngitis and the only part I played was swelling the first-night audience by 25 per cent.

To be honest, I never did share my fellow players' enthusiasm for the haphazard co-op – ten of us in a condemned basement flat – that existed that chilly August. I was, as my mother had pointed out, a bit old for it. At twenty-six, with one career behind me (corporate bank, I'm afraid; I was first in the queue for voluntary redundancies when they restructured), I had decided to return to the bohemian life of my student days for a while with my lump sum. I had been in one of the less successful Footlights tours when I was at Cambridge. Five years on I hadn't realized how softened by expenses-paid business trips I had become. Communal living and expressing myself through drama were not quite as attractive as I had remembered.

I returned to London in style – the flight alone cost as much as the previous month's existence – but wasn't aware how much champagne I had consumed until I rang my mother from Heathrow (she always worries about me flying) and burst into tears.

It seems oddly defeatist to admit that the next week

was one of the happiest I have ever spent. Tucked under nice clean sheets and blankets (why did duvets ever become so popular?), flowery curtains flapping and Pinner church bells ringing in through the windows of my childhood bedroom, hot lemon drinks made with real lemon and honey, because my mother had read an article somewhere that said paracetamol could be harmful, and, when I got my voice back, some ordinary, non-theatrical chats with Mum. I almost forgot that there was a world outside in which I had a flat with a real mortgage, a number of friends with expectations of me, and a future.

Mum was right, I should have taken a typing course, because if I had I would have been able to work for a more lucrative outfit than Office Secs. But then I might never have met Agatha Brown.

2

'You were the cheapest we could find,' she said, after the initial good-morning.

I said I wasn't surprised. My qualifications were not up to the standards required, as I had found out to my humiliation the week before when I had taken typing tests at all the well-known agencies and been rejected on speed and accuracy. Never having failed an exam before, this had been a blow, but I had eventually found my way to a dingy office in an alley off the Charing Cross Road where an agency called Office Secs advertised 'no previous experience required'. I was slightly suspicious, but forced myself to ring the bell and the Australian woman, who appeared to be running the business alone, leapt at my CV because of my knowledge of theatre and sent me to Brown and Brown. I was to be the managing director's PA for three months while her real secretary was on maternity leave.

I started to say that, while my speeds were perhaps not up to normal standards, I would ensure the work was done, but she interrupted me.

'No need to go into the boring detail, darling. I know you will be more than adequate. I can tell as soon as someone walks through that door whether I will like them. And I like you. I've been in this business long enough to know at a glance whether I will get on with someone.'

I felt somewhat equivocal about this friendliness. I

didn't know whether I actually wanted to be liked on first sight by my new boss. I had never been a secretary before and I was not sure what the nature of the relationship should be. More importantly, I felt that my appearance, which was the only way she could possibly judge me, gave no indication of my personality. I had bought a rather ordinary blue-and-white-spotted dress to wear on my first day especially because of its anonymity.

'It was the shoes, I suppose,' said Agatha, as if answering my unspoken doubt.

I was wearing magenta suede pumps designed by a university friend who had recently been featured in *Vogue* and had since become unaffordable.

'Miranda Moss. I have a pair in turquoise and one in yellow. Except I never seem to wear the yellow,' she added somewhat forlornly.

I agreed that yellow often seemed like a good idea in the shop but always, somehow, turned out to be a mistake. She disagreed about the always, revealing that one of her all-time favourite dresses (but she said frock) was a yellow taffeta New Look original with a lemon crinoline that one wouldn't have imagined could work, but emphatically did. I tried to picture her in it.

'But not, surely, with yellow shoes?' I ventured.

'Of course not,' she replied, quite sharply, and picked up her phone to take a call.

I looked around Agatha Brown's office in some awe. A large Victorian desk sat between two floor-to-ceiling Georgian windows looking over Soho rooftops (we were on the third floor). The curtains were thick red silk velvet showing the signs of many years of swishing, the floor, an assembly of Persian rugs. One side wall was entirely lined with books, mostly plays and programmes,

4

the other was a collage of posters, telegrams and cards, like a gigantic pinboard. Dusty-ribbon rosettes, the remnants of bouquets sent over many years, interspersed the messages of thanks, first-night photographs and reviews from newspapers all over the world. In one leather armchair a huge tabby cat slept. I had taken it for a cushion until it stirred and began to snore. Scripts lay in piles all over the floor and on the strangely incongruous 1950s fake leopardskin sofa. On an occasional table a bubble lamp in purple and orange blobbed away silently, taking me back to one of those dazzlingly clear memories of childhood.

One of the last memories I have of my father before he left us is of him and me walking down the Portobello Road market. It was a wintry dark afternoon and one of the stalls was lit up with a display of those lamps, which were such an emblem of modern living then. I can still hear the hum of the generator as I stood and watched, mesmerized by their oily artificial light. I remember wishing that we were the sort of family who would have a lamp like that on our television set; the sort of family who would eat fish fingers and Arctic roll; and I would have a Sindy doll to play with. I remember standing there desperately wanting to be ordinary. Of course, when he went away, and I no longer had to eat vegetarian food or make potato prints, the advertised delights of normal family life paled somewhat, and whenever I see one of those bubble lights, I'm filled with a strange sensation of guilt, seeing again my father's admonitory glance as he took my hand and pulled me firmly towards the stall that sold loose lentils by the pound.

'Now, Sophie, if I may. You must call me Agatha, of course. There's quite a lot to be done. First, you find the kitchen and make us a pot of camomile tea. Then we'll have a gossip.'

But since she was on the phone constantly until she went out to lunch and didn't return until after four-thirty, we didn't have our gossip that day. I spent the rest of the morning opening the post and familiarizing myself with the client list.

Brown and Brown was a long-established theatrical agency set up by Agatha and her sister, Dorothy, in the late 1950s. They were the first agents to handle clients in all aspects of theatre – directors, actors, playwrights and later designers too. I asked the other secretary, Janet, with whom I shared a corridor, what had happened to Dorothy, but she shot me a warning glance and whispered that she would tell me at lunchtime.

We took our sandwiches to a bench in Soho Square. It was a beautiful September day. She explained, as we munched, that it was wiser not to mention the other Miss Brown in the office. She had heard there'd been a massive falling-out over a double-booking years ago and Dorothy had been pushed out. She had subsequently married a client of Agatha and the rift had never been healed. Agatha had made their book-keeper, who was called Anthony – never Tony, she warned – White, her partner. According to Janet, Agatha completely dominated him. Although he was now a director of the company, Agatha refused to change its name (not surprisingly, I thought, since it would then be Brown and White, which sounded a bit silly) and was very mean about allowing him to buy shares. I wondered how Janet had access to this sort of information. From the way she spoke about Anthony, I thought that perhaps her relationship with him was rather closer than secretarial. She began to describe his clients, whom she said made more

6

money than Agatha's, even though they had less snob value. I asked why, if he had such a bad deal, he didn't leave and set up his own agency. Janet just sniffed and said that Agatha was a very powerful woman.

I remarked that I had found her rather enjoyable and straightforward that morning.

'But you're no threat, you see,' said Janet. 'She's a nightmare to deal with, a real old-style battleaxe. I suppose,' she added, 'that's why she is so good at the job. She's quite incapable of any human feelings. The only things she loves are her job and her cat.'

I inquired about Vivienne, the woman whose job I was doing.

'Poor Viv. She's had to put up with the Ag for two years. She was just about to look for another job, when she discovered she was pregnant. It seemed daft not to get her maternity leave paid for, so she decided to stay. I will say for Agatha, she's good on rights, but she was furious with Viv. Jealousy, I think. She's given her life to work and she's way past childbearing now. She said she couldn't imagine why Viv would want to bring another helpless being into this terrible world – that's how she put it – but Viv and I think she wouldn't be so fond of that cat if she didn't have any maternal instincts at all.'

I felt a peculiar twinge of sympathy for Miss Brown, who had so spontaneously expressed her liking for me when I walked in nervously, but I decided to suspend any judgement. I didn't want to like, or not like, anyone at Brown and Brown. It was, after all, a job just to keep me going, until I decided what I really wanted to do.

I was kept very busy that afternoon, mostly on the phone, with inquiries from advertising agencies about actors' availability. I discovered that there was a hand-coloured calendar in each file with their movements meticulously mapped out in a complicated colour scheme for booked, provisionally booked and various shades of resting. I wrestled with typing a couple of invoices and chased up a well-known West End theatre for overdue royalties. A lot of time was spent ferrying pots of herbal tea from the kitchen to my employer.

I have taken little interest in herbal tea since my childhood, when it was obligatory. My father refused to allow products containing caffeine into our home. He was (and still is, I imagine) an irrational man who bans coffee and yet smokes a packet of untipped Gauloises every day. My mother and I have eschewed health-food shops since his departure. I was therefore unprepared for the array of bright, attractively designed packets in the small kitchen at the agency, and when Agatha asked me to bring her a pot of Cherry Pickers, I thought at first that it was the name of a script she had mislaid. I was so tempted by the warming names that I even decided to try a cup of Golden Ginseng Glory myself, but felt rather let down by its stale, self-righteous flavour after all the life-enhancing blurb on the box.

Five-thirty arrived very quickly and Agatha called me in to her office.

'Must apologize for today,' she said. 'Had hoped to get something dictated. Has it been too boring?'

I assured her that it hadn't, that in fact I had found it rather a thrill dealing with people whose work I admired. She beamed and told me how refreshing it was to have someone who understood about the theatre.

'Most temps have no idea,' she said. 'Have a whisky.'

I had arranged a drink with a friend, so made my excuses. As I left the office I heard her uncorking the

Glenmorangie and saying, 'Well, darling, it looks like a taxi for us again tonight.'

I assumed she was speaking to the cat.

3

Martin is the man my mother thinks I should marry. We met on the first day of the graduate trainee scheme at the bank and have been friends ever since. He probably is the person I should marry, but we only ever discuss it when we are both getting drunk after one or other of us has finished a relationship. The form is that one of us says something like 'Oh God, we get on so well together, why don't we just put an end to all this suffering and get married?' Then we have another bottle of Chardonnay and cry a bit more. Then he pours me into a taxi and finds his own way home to Wandsworth. I rather suspect that he takes the last train, because he is a bit tight with money and not really given to extravagant gestures; and that, and the fact that he really does seem to like living in Wandsworth, means that, whether we should or not, we will never be a couple. But I do love him dearly.

He did a bit of a double-take at my secretary's outfit when I walked down the spiral staircase of the Garrick Street Wine Bar. In my days at the bank I had always affected a power-dressing style. High heels, short-skirted suits in bright colours and lots of gold-effect jewellery. I always like to look the part, and banking was by far the toughest role I have attempted. Martin was the only person there with a sense of humour and he saw through the fake Chanel exterior straight away. I used to do my hair in a French pleat because I thought it made me look older and fiercer, but bits of it always seemed to escape when Martin was around.

'Very demure,' he said, as I sat down, and asked the waiter for another glass. 'Sophie, what are you up to? I mean, "Take a letter, Miss Fitt", it's not really you, is it?'

'They use dictaphones nowadays, actually, and, as a matter of fact, if every day is like today, I'm going to enjoy my job. Which is more than you do, after all.'

'But the money . . .'

'It's enough to get by. I quite like not having any responsibility. My lunch today was a sandwich, not three indigestible courses opposite some lech selling something I didn't believe in, and my boss is an eccentric 1950s throwback with a tabby cat, not some yuppie upstart in the latest Armani.'

'All right, all right.' He held up his palms in defence. 'What's she like, then, this Agatha Brown?'

'Well, apparently universally feared, but I quite liked her.' I recounted our meeting and imitated her way of speaking, which was aristocratic English with a touch of American hip. She seemed to me to come from that peculiarly confident breed of upper-class Englishwomen who in another decade might have flown aeroplanes solo or travelled alone up the Amazon and written books about it. I supposed she must have been in her fifties, but she could almost have been any age above forty-five. She was tall and angular with a striking face that could have been very beautiful if she had been less intelligent and more graceful. As it was, she had presence. Her clothes could have been *haute couture* or bought at a jumble sale – I suspected a combination of the two – and her hair was absolutely white and was cut in a Louise Brooks bob which fell rather helmet-like around her intense face.

'She has enormous style,' I said, 'and I think it will be

fun working there. It's fascinating to see another side to the theatre.'

'So, the career in acting is over?' he asked.

'Inasmuch as it ever started. I don't think I've got the right temperament for it.'

'What do you mean? I don't know many people who'd be prepared to stand up in front of a pub full of people and tell jokes,' said Martin.

'Oh, I've got the confidence all right.' I do a stand-up gig upstairs in a pub in Islington once a month. 'It's just that I hate actors,' I said, and drained my glass.

Martin roared with laughter.

'Two months ago, you were saying that you longed to be with people who were sensitive and creative.'

'Well, I did. I just didn't realize what a load of egocentric bores they were. What about your love life?'

I was anxious to change the subject, as I had felt a bit of a failure at Edinburgh. Martin obliged me with a story about trying to ask out the woman who lives in the flat above his. I have never met her but I'm sure I'm right in thinking that she will never be Martin's girlfriend. He has harboured a passion for her from the day she moved in and he offered to give her a hand with her trunk. Ever since then he has acted as removal man, electrician, twenty-four-hour bank and shoulder to cry on, but he has yet to kiss her. Martin says that she is very shy, but since she is an air hostess and seems to have a different boyfriend every time she is back in the country, I find this hard to believe. I am not as sympathetic as I should be because I think it is very clichéd of him to fancy an air hostess and very unadventurous in that she is also, in effect, the girl next door. I can never really believe he is serious.

'Well, since you're affecting a look of glazed boredom, why don't you recount details of your latest, Soph?'

'Nothing.'

'Have another glass of wine.'

'Oh, all right. You know the actors I was talking about?'

'The egocentric bores?'

'Yup. Well, I fell for one in Edinburgh. I knew him a bit at college. He has been quite successful – you know, walk-on part in *Casualty*, coffee advert, that kind of thing – very good-looking etc., etc., and straight. Well, we had a deep and meaningful conversation one night when everyone else was down the pub, and he suddenly said, "Sophie, why don't we just do it, do it, here on the cushions?"

'I looked around the room. It was like some sit-com parody of a 1960s commune with bean bags and a filthy brown carpet. Call me bourgeois, call me old-fashioned, but I just couldn't bring myself to "do it" there, so I suggested we went to a hotel for the night. Well, of course, it's not so easy to get a hotel in the middle of Edinburgh during the Festival. I hadn't thought of that. We ended up getting a taxi out to a travel lodge near the motorway – very salubrious . . . It was beginning to feel a bit awkward, once the spontaneity had gone, and as soon as we got there, he started muttering about how threatened he felt by my credit card, my career at the bank, my haircut. Christ, I only wanted a fuck and I had three hours of his pseudo-psychology. I said that to him, in a jokey kind of way –'

'What? You said what?'

'Well, I just said that I thought we had come for a fuck, not a fucking primal scream. That was the end of that, of course. No sense of humour at all. He told me I wasn't a sharing person and borrowed £10 of my emasculating money to get a taxi back to the bean bags. I stayed the night by myself, since I had paid for it.

'I emptied the mini-bar and watched *American Gladiators* on TV. I quite enjoyed myself, actually.'

'So, what happened after that?'

'Well, I apologized, because I thought I should, I'm not sure why, and we behaved as if nothing had happened. Which it hadn't, so that was quite easy. I never saw my £10 again, of course. It would have been so very "unsharing" of me to ask for it . . . Don't know what it is about me and men. How can someone be threatened by a haircut?'

'Well, I preferred you with long hair.'

'Oh, for God's sake, Martin!' As part of changing my life, I had recently had my long hair cut very short, so short it had to be shaved at the back of the neck to get the line right. I loved it and secretly thought it made me look rather attractively gamine, but nobody else seemed to agree. 'You sound like my mother.'

'Well,' said Martin, 'your mother is very beautiful.'

And that was her undoing. My mother is very beautiful and always has been. When she was six, she won a competition to be photographed for a soap advert and her face was seen in every women's magazine in England. Years later, at the beginning of the swinging 1960s, she was waitressing in a coffee shop in Soho, her only act of rebellion having been to refuse to go to secretarial college as her parents had wished, when a moderately successful artist she had served asked her to model for him. In her nice innocent way she accepted, and quite soon after they were married. My mother is very beautiful. She has a heart-shaped, heart-breaking face. She is also the kind of daft woman who would marry an artist after modelling for him just because he said he loved her. The artist, of course, was my father. I like to think that their relationship peaked, inasmuch as it was capable of peaking, at the moment of my conception, which was probably within about twelve hours of her serving him with a cappuccino.

Which is not to say that she is a bimbo. She is a thoroughly suburban woman with a beautiful face who is infinitely happier in Pinner than in Soho. And it isn't to say that he didn't try to be a good father. I'm sure he did try. After all, he stayed with us for six years before disappearing with another waitress to Paris. I haven't seen him since.

I told Martin about my week of blissful recuperation with Mum and gave him her love. I didn't tell him that she had also spent several hours sitting on the side of my bed talking about Martin's good points in comparison to the amorphous group she referred to as my 'other men'. I think that my mother suspects I got in with a very shady crowd at Cambridge because I never took any of my boyfriends home. The reason was that I wasn't as confident then and I didn't know what those assured ex-public schoolboys would make of our villa in Pinner. I preferred to remain enigmatic about my background, which is probably why none of those relationships got very far. When my mother came up to Cambridge to see me graduate (her only invitation) she was an instant success. She had chosen to wear a fitted buttercup-yellow linen suit which would have been a disaster on anyone less slim, but made her look, especially in contrast with the uniformly black-clad students and the other mums in their voluminous Monsoon dresses, as fresh as the garden daisies she had artfully pinned to her white straw hat. After she had drunk a couple of glasses of Pimm's, her awed nervousness disappeared and she was persuaded into a punt, where she reclined for the rest of the day, not seeming to mind that she was displaying rather a lot of leg, and asked the occasional undemanding question about the history of Cambridge which made me wince with embarrassment, but seemed to charm the men in attendance.

Since Cambridge nobody has lasted long enough to be taken home, except Jerry, and, well, that was impossible. So really the only man my mother has ever seen me with regularly has been Martin, and whenever I tell her that nothing is going on, she just smiles knowingly, which annoys me no end.

My friends are always surprised when they meet my mother, because she and I are so different. It is not so much our looks – we both have blonde hair and blue eyes and, although I cannot compete with her beauty, I am a rather lesser version of her – but our personalities are complete opposites. She is gentle and equable with no imagination whatsoever. I am what romantic novels like to call feisty and what my mother likes to call difficult. I am very rarely settled and am often irritable and spiky. This is why people who meet my mother generally prefer her to me. This has happened all my life, so I am used to it, but I did at that moment want to hit Martin, who was meant to be my friend, for his dreamy expression as he contemplated those two icons of femininity, my mother and the air hostess. I decided we had better call it a night.

4

I hadn't seen my flat for over a month, and it looked as if I wouldn't be seeing it that night either, as the light in the hall failed to work and I suspected we had been cut off. I own the top-floor flat above a launderette in a terrace of shops in Primrose Hill.

There was a fire in the building a couple of years before I moved in which gutted it. The people who run the launderette bought the building with the intention of doing the whole thing up and selling off the three flats above. Fortunately for me, they put a new roof on and revamped the top floor, but they had overestimated the number of service-washes they could do and ran out of money. The two floors below me remain derelict and the whole house shakes through the night as wash after wash is completed on the ground floor. I sometimes dream that my floor collapses and I sink gently down to street level and end up being spun in the top-loading dryer downstairs. I had the flat surveyed, of course, when I bought it, and my surveyor advised me strongly not to buy. But then he was Reg, my mother's long-time boy-friend, and I thought he was being unnecessarily cautious, as usual. So I went ahead, because I loved the place, and I haven't regretted it. Much.

I waded my way through four weeks' junk mail and groped my way up three flights of stairs to my door. Having fumbled for ages with the keys, I reached for the switch inside and, like a miracle, the lights in my flat came on. I realized that I hadn't spoken to Costas about the communal charges for some time, but I had paid my own bills to date and had been rewarded. As Reg had pointed out, it was a ridiculous flat as an investment, because very few people would want to buy it, if I wanted to sell. It consists of one large room with a kitchen at one end, a smallish bedroom and a very ugly bathroom. But I couldn't resist it because the living room has floor-to-ceiling windows at the front and there are french doors on to a roof terrace, which is as large as the flat itself, at the back. I have put up trellises (or, to be fair, Martin put up trellises) all round with vines and wistaria growing on them and I spend as much time as the weather allows sitting outside in my garden looking over the rooftops. Apart from the traffic and washing machines, the only sound I hear is the barking of sea lions in London Zoo.

I found a bottle of tonic water in the fridge, along with some unrecognizable bits of food that I had forgotten to throw out before I left for Edinburgh, poured myself a very strong gin and tonic and went outside to sit in the darkness and think about life. I decided that I felt the freest I had ever felt and I drank a toast to Office Secs.

I realized the next morning that I shouldn't have been quite so enthusiastic in my celebrations. I arrived at the office on time but only because I had caught a taxi, something I had vowed to cut out in my new austerity. When Agatha arrived, brandishing a tape to be typed, it took me half an hour to work out how to use the playback machine and six sheets of paper before it dawned on me that there was a self-correcting button on the typewriter. Janet was off with a cold and so there was no one to offer advice. I also had to take all incoming calls and at ten-thirty Anthony White went into Agatha's office to protest that he had been cut off a dozen times. I thought I was about to get the sack when Agatha called me into her office.

'I say,' she said, 'what month is it now?'

'September,' I ventured.

'Good,' she said. 'That means we can have oysters. Are you doing anything for lunch?'

Grand Central Oyster Bar had only recently opened but it had received a rave write-up in the *Sunday Times* and was swarming with customers. Even Agatha's haughty aplomb could not get us a table, so we sat at the semi-circular bar and tried to make ourselves heard above the din. She ordered a Whisky Sour and I a large bottle of mineral water. Agatha's manner was direct and it didn't take me long to appreciate that her interest in having lunch with me was the same as her interest in any lunch. Business. She wanted information about my peers.

She insisted that we each have a dozen oysters and my stomach sank a little, partly at the prospect of eating them (I felt I could just have managed six) and partly at the prospect of justifying the rather exaggerated accounts of my acting at Cambridge that she had obviously read in my CV. I managed to drop a few names and regaled her with accounts of the politics of the Footlights. In the end I ran out of material and was forced to admit to my dabblings on the comic fringe, which interested her greatly. She made me promise to tell her when my next slot was so that she could come along. I told her that it was really only a bit of fun, but she dismissed this, saying that most of the new successful sit-coms had emanated from stand-up routines on the fringe. I found it rather refreshing that someone of her calibre and age should still be interested in new material and started to say so.

'Good grief, Sophie, you make me sound as if I have passed my sell-by date! In this business you can never ignore talent. Think about Joe Orton and Peggy Ramsay – some of the brightest stars just walk in from the street. You have to invest all the time, never get complacent. Anyway, it's much more fun dealing with raw talent.' She tipped up an oyster and drank the juice. 'Actors and writers get terribly self-obsessed after a very short time. I have to have some new ones or I would end up killing some of the neurotic old breadwinners.'

I laughed, but she seemed perfectly serious.

'The sad thing is,' she said, 'the more involved you get, the less they thank you for it when they make it. You devote your life to wanting them to succeed and then, when they do, you become redundant. You'll meet one of them this afternoon. He's a beautiful untouched idealist from Derry – inasmuch as you can be untouched if you've grown up in Derry – mesmerizing actor and not a bad writer at all. Quite delicious to look at. I expect that he'll become a dreadful bore too once he's had his name in lights.'

I said I was surprised how cynical she sounded.

'Ah yes, but we're all kept going by the idea that one of these days we will be proved wrong, aren't we?'

I said I had spent five years doing exactly that at the bank. Every Sunday as I geared myself up to go into work the next morning I would tell myself that it could only get better. That if I made vice-president level by the time I was thirty, then I would get a company car, a huge pension entitlement etc., etc. But then one Sunday I realized that I had no need of a car. I couldn't even drive and four years was too long a time to waste doing a job I hated. I cursed the day I had conned myself into thinking that I was one of Thatcher's children and, if I couldn't beat them, I should join them. But I knew that I would never be able to pay my mortgage if I left my job with its huge mortgage subsidy.

'So how did you manage?' Agatha asked.

'Well, I was lucky. The next week the bank announced that there were going to be cut-backs. They meant at a more menial level, I think, but I suppose they had to ask the entire workforce for voluntary redundancies. When I got to work, all the really ambitious ones who used to arrive at seven o'clock in the morning had been worrying for two hours. When they told me the news I leapt in the air with joy, sought out my boss and offered my resignation on the spot. I was out the same day with enough cash in hand to be able to take the dreadful wages you offer and not worry for a few months, until I decide what I really want to do.'

She smiled at the mention of the wages.

'And what is it that you really want to do?'

'That's my problem. I'd like to do something creative, but wouldn't we all? Maybe you have the ideal combination of business and art, but after what you've just said . . .'

'Well, perhaps I exaggerated.' She smiled. 'I love the job really. I have given up an awful lot to do it.'

'Like?'

'Far too many things to go into here, darling. We should be getting back to work. Thank you for your company. It has been most enjoyable. And I am lucky you gave up that horrid job.'

On the staircase up to the office Agatha lagged behind, obviously finding the climb difficult. I walked back down to see what was wrong. She had paled and was gripping her side as if in pain.

'You go on ahead, darling. I'll be with you in a second,' she said.

'Are you OK?'

'Just a little *crise de foie* – I always think that sounds religious, don't you? I think the food was perhaps a touch rich.'

'Could I bring you some water or anything?' I asked, as she sat down wearily on the polished wooden stairs.

'No, no. Go on.'

I went upstairs on my own and was greeted by Anthony White. Although I sat directly on the route between his office and Agatha's, and he had passed me several times, he had not bothered to acknowledge me since I arrived at the office. There always seemed to be an atmosphere of impatience surrounding him, as if he had too much to do and not enough time. To introduce himself to a mere temp would have wasted several precious seconds. He was rather a stocky man, with wiry greying hair that looked as if it had been cut in the same style since the 1970s. His clothes were obviously expensive, but he had no real style. The Paul Smith jacket was slightly too long for him and served only to make him look fat. Nobody seemed to have told him that you shouldn't wear a striped tie with a striped shirt.

'Do you have the time?' he asked politely. His voice was so incongruously plummy, it made me suspect elocution lessons.

I looked at my watch.

'About a quarter to four,' I answered straightforwardly, not realizing that there was another agenda. This seemed to infuriate him and his manner changed in an instant from excessive charm to knife-like aggression.

'Who, exactly, do you think you are?' he said. 'Do you really think that we are going to tolerate a temp taking a three-hour lunch-break? Especially when there are no other staff in today. Agatha tells me that you're a graduate. Well, that may impress her, but it doesn't make the slightest difference to me. The lunch-break is one hour for you. Any longer and you're out. Consider yourself warned.'

I was so shocked that I couldn't speak for several seconds. I hadn't been spoken to like this since I was once caught buying sherbet fountains in the local sweet shop, when I should have been in the playground at primary school. I was just opening my mouth to retaliate when the phone rang beside me.

I picked up the receiver and pressed the button to connect the call. It was a client of Agatha. I took a message, then turned to face Anthony White.

'I have actually been having lunch with Miss Brown,' I said in my coolest and most patronizing voice. 'I'm sorry if you've been troubled. If I can help at all, do let me know, but I prefer to be asked in a civil way.'

It was his turn to stare at me with his mouth open. He was trying to muster some cutting reply when Agatha appeared at the door.

'You'll really have to get your own temp, Anthony,' she said, I felt deliberately misinterpreting the situation, 'if Janet's going to be away for any time. Sophie has quite enough to get on with for me.'

'Including long lunches, I suppose,' he said under his breath, and turned back to his office and slammed the door.

I looked rather nervously at Agatha. I didn't want to be the cause of disagreements between her and her partner, but I felt that I wasn't really to blame. She gave me a large wink and then followed Anthony into his office, slamming the door equally loudly behind her.

I decided to get on with the tape which Agatha had given me that morning. There were a couple of letters of congratulation to directors whose new work had just been previewed and a note acknowledging a script that had been sent in. After that the dictation seemed to stop, but I neglected to switch off the foot pedal and as I was typing the envelopes I started to hear noises through the headphones.

First of all a swooshing noise, then a rustling, then a long sigh. The tape went silent for several minutes. Then suddenly Agatha's voice shouted, 'Get off!'

Then, 'Oh, I'm sorry, darling, I didn't mean to shout at you! Come here, my sweet, and let me stroke you.'

Then, 'That's my dinner, darling. I'm sorry, I forgot to get you anything. Let me see. I'll look in the fridge . . . Ahh, now would you like some smoked salmon? Yes? That's much nicer than Whiskas, isn't it?'

At this point I realized that Agatha had left the dictaphone tape on by mistake and was talking to her cat.

I was going to mention it but never got the chance that afternoon, as the young actor from Derry arrived to distract me.

5

His name was Gregory Murtagh and he had a face like a Caravaggio cherub. His hair was blue-black, curly and collar-length. He wore it parted at the side, so that long, glossy curls fell over his face as he talked and he constantly swept them back with his left hand. I had an immediate urge to tie his hair back with an elastic band so that my eyes could linger on his beautiful face for more than a few seconds at a time. His skin was absolutely white, but not unhealthily so, and his eyes were clear brown, huge and fringed with black lashes. He smiled infrequently but when he did his face transformed from a kind of serene, almost feminine, beauty to the mischief of a Puck-like child, knowing and yet innocent, indulged and supremely sensual.

I hadn't heard him come in and was trying to find his file in a filing cabinet when I sensed someone behind me. I turned round. He was very tall and thin, with an endearing stoop which made me feel, for some reason, as if he was standing almost indecently close to me.

'I'm Greg,' he said. His accent made his name seem as if it had at least two syllables.

'I'm Sophie,' I replied. 'I'm working here at the moment.'

'So I see.' He smiled. I melted.

I felt I ought to offer him coffee, or tea, and ask him to take a seat until Agatha was ready to see him, but I hated the idea of appearing to be in a menial position to someone who was my age or less. Still, this was all part of the job, I reminded myself.

'D'you fancy a coffee?' I finally said, as if he were a friend who had just dropped round to my flat.

'I'd love one,' he replied, 'but only if I can get it.'

I felt slightly alarmed that he had sensed my discomfort, and raised an eyebrow.

'It's just that the coffee here is truly awful,' he said. 'Agatha doesn't drink it and so she buys the cheapest instant for other people. You've noticed? There's a great Italian place round the corner. I usually bring one with me, but I forgot.' He took my order and reappeared after a couple of minutes with two steaming cappuccinos in polystyrene cups. I sat down with him in the capacious, battered leather chairs in the waiting area and we began to chat.

Greg had been in London for only a few weeks. He had landed a part in a drama documentary about the Maguire Seven which was shooting on location in Kilburn. During his free time Agatha was getting him auditions, which was why, he said, he popped into the office quite a lot. They had first met in Dublin, where he had lived since university. She had been to a performance of *Krapp's Last Tape* in the Beckett Festival at the Gate and had come backstage afterwards to congratulate him. He had heard that she was in town. Dublin was such a small town, he said, that the visit of an agent was news, but he hadn't imagined that someone as eminent as she was would have the slightest interest in him.

'I was bowled over.' He smiled his wicked smile. 'But I hear you're an actress too.'

'Not really,' I said. It occurred to me only later that this was an odd piece of information for him to have, since I was sure that Agatha had more pressing things to discuss with him than the provenance of her temp. 'I do a stand-up act in a pub sometimes, but that's about it.'

'What, telling jokes?'

I nodded.

'How strange that people are so different from the way they look,' he said.

'What do you mean?' I asked, laughing.

'Well, you look so fragile and sweet-tempered. Most of the comediennes I know are terrible fat old dykes.'

'I suppose I should take that as a compliment,' I said. We seemed to be beginning to flirt with each other, which was fine by me.

'I suppose you should.'

At which point Agatha appeared in the door and beckoned him in. She looked at me rather quizzically. I realized that I had assumed a relaxed position with my shoes kicked off and my feet tucked under my bum.

'I'll have some Rosehip, Sophie. And Greg?' she inquired, re-establishing the hierarchy.

'Oh, let's not bother,' he said. 'Why don't we just go for a glass at the pub?'

She looked at him with an amused expression, trying at first to be stern but very soon capitulating in the face of his twinkly charm.

'Oh, you bloody Irishmen!' she said, and went back into her office to collect her coat. He helped her with it most solicitously and guided her to the office entrance with his hand on the small of her back.

She was so animated and he so attentive that they both forgot to say goodbye. I sniffed, rather pointedly, and detected a strong waft of Diorissimo.

6

I was beginning to think that I wouldn't have any
material at all for my show when I ran into Stephanie.

The first week of my new job had been more exhaust-
ing than I could have imagined. I had, foolishly in
retrospect, swallowed my pride and made my peace with
Mr White, or Anthony, as he now insisted I call him,
after our little contretemps over lunch. Since Janet's cold
appeared to have developed into flu, she had called in
sick for the rest of the week and I felt it would be a
politic gesture to help her boss out. I found myself
working late a couple of nights running. Irritatingly, he
seemed incapable of leaving the office before I did, and
on Thursday evening stood, shifting from foot to foot,
looking over my shoulder for a good half-hour while I
typed before asking me out, as if it were some sort of
reward, for a drink. I declined, pleading a tenants'
meeting at home, whereupon he insisted on giving me a
lift. He lived in Hertfordshire, he said, and it was on his
way to the A1.

He kept his car in an NCP on St Martin's Lane and
we had to wait several minutes while the attendants
brought it down in a lift. Never having owned a car
myself, I was amazed by this procedure and remarked
that it was the sort of thing one expected in New York
but not London. He smiled, as if gratified by such an
impressionable companion. When the car finally arrived,
it was exactly as I would have predicted had we been

playing that dinner-party game, 'If he were a car/meal/colour etc., what would he be?' A metallic-grey, two-seater, Japanese sports car that made an awful lot of noise, even though we never got up any real speed between the West End and Camden. It seemed to me that Anthony was exactly the sort of man who would have liked to own a Ferrari but could never, quite, afford one.

We chatted awkwardly. He told me he was divorced, with a twelve-year-old son whom he tried to see as often as he could, which was why he still lived near his wife. I remarked that it was a long journey to do every day, which gave him his cue to say, patting the steering wheel, 'It doesn't really feel that far in this!'

I made the appropriate appreciative noises but I felt it was an undignified car for a man in his fifties and, as he roared away up Primrose Hill, the fleeting thought 'mutton dressed as lamb' passed through my mind and made me smile.

There wasn't, of course, a tenants' meeting but I did bump into Costas outside my door and we went to the local taverna, owned by one of his cousins, and had far too much retsina to drink, while we discussed our joint responsibility for light bulbs on the staircase.

Which was another reason why I was in a bit of a daze as I wandered around Camden Sainsbury's on Friday night, trying to decide what to buy to eat at the weekend.

Stephanie accosted me at the ready-meals section and advised me of the delights of fresh tagliatelli with tomato and mascarpone sauce, and I felt obliged to invite her to eat it with me. She contributed a bag of continental salad and half a cucumber, which she picked at all evening whilst drinking litre after litre of still mineral water.

Stephanie had lived next door to me in hall during our first year at Cambridge. When she arrived she was a big-boned, sporty-looking girl with a fresh complexion and lots of girls' public-school *bonhomie*. By the end of the first year she had become a neurotic waif with an eating disorder bordering on anorexia. Cambridge did that to some people. I tended to avoid her after I moved out of college, because I found the whole experience of university made me anxious enough without a constant discussion of calories and metabolic functions.

I hadn't seen her for several years, but had learned from mutual acquaintances that she had moved to Camden and so it was not much of a surprise to encounter her under the bright revealing neon of Sainsbury's. She had managed to keep the model-like figure she yearned for and it was accentuated by tight black leggings and a waist-length designer version of a biker's jacket which revealed no thighs or posterior at all.

What I had not envisaged as I offered my casual dinner invitation was that Stephanie, now content in her body, had grown impatient with her soul and seemed to have tried as many life-changing courses in the last few years as she had diets at Cambridge. I suppose I had been expecting a gentle, gossipy girls' evening. What I got was a psycho-babble inquisition.

'You're looking very well,' I began, as I boiled a saucepan of water for the pasta.

'You're not,' she replied. 'Oh, don't get me wrong, you look fine . . . but there's something about your aura.'

'I've got a bit of a hangover, if that's what you mean.'

'No, no, more fundamental than that. I mean, you don't seem happy with yourself. Sorry to be direct, but I have learned that it is very useful to be direct.'

'Or rude?' I joked.

'Ah, now, I was right. Otherwise you wouldn't be so defensive,' she continued earnestly.

'Oh, for God's sake, Steph, you're beginning to sound like a shrink in a dreadful soap opera.'

'What makes you say dreadful when you're talking about shrinks? Have you ever thought about that?' she said, ever so seriously.

'I was actually talking about the quality of the soap opera, rather than the shrink,' I replied. 'Come on, lighten up, as they say, and get yourself a drink.'

'I don't drink any more.'

My heart sank. I was just coming to the nice bit of the hangover when the insistent headache lifts and you feel you really would be doing yourself good to have a glass of something fortifying, like Rioja. I decided to ignore her and poured myself a tumbler. We took our plates of pasta and the salad on to the terrace and for a moment she reverted to the well-mannered middle-class girl she was and commented on the vines and the flowers and how nice it all was. I took a slug of red wine.

'It's great to relax after the week I've had,' I said, lighting a couple of candles on the metal table and sipping my Rioja.

'Do you find you need alcohol to relax?' she asked.

'I don't know about need,' I said, 'but I like it.'

'Ah,' she said, and gulped her Evian.

I started to count up in my head the number of drinks I had had in the last week. There were rather more than the total suggested as safe in an article I had read some time ago on the *Guardian* Women's Page, but, I told myself, it had been a hard week.

'Do you find yourself making excuses for the amount you drink?' she continued.

'Well . . .'

It was like doing one of those quizzes in *Cosmopolitan*. Are You an Alcoholic? Are You Good in Bed? That sort of thing.

I tried to laugh it off, but Stephanie pressed on.

'Do you drink to forget?' she asked.

'I can't remember,' I said.

My problem is (if you can call it a problem – I see it more as one of the nicer sides of my character) that I simply can't bring myself to be horrible to people like Stephanie. I allowed her to sit on my beautiful roof terrace and criticize every aspect of my character for several hours. I like to think I would have told her to shut up earlier if I hadn't, on the second glass of Rioja, had the glimmerings of a new persona for my act.

My 'act' began, I suppose, at a Christmas party at the bank. We were all sitting at tables with our 'teams' (extraordinary management-speak for small groups of highly competitive people who were meant to work together to further the profits of the bank), wearing paper hats extracted from extremely expensive designer crackers. The atmosphere was about as festive as the reading of a will, but more secretive, since everyone was individually trying to work out the relative size of his or her bonus. We all ate our perfect escalopes of turkey resting in a port and cranberry coulis, and our side-plates of baby vegetables; we toyed with our individual Christmas puddings and drank the fine wines from the correct glasses arrayed in front of us. I was trying to hold a conversation with the team member next to me, an American wearing red braces (or suspenders, as he called them) whose name was Randolph Brooks the Fourth. He had irritated me all year with his unleavened ambition, but rather than challenge him I found myself, unconsciously at first, imitating him. My accent grew more and more American and my speech pattern slowed. It was as if I was, in my boredom, transforming myself into him. (Try saying 'My friends call me Randy,' with no trace of irony in your voice.) When Martin and I slunk off early to the nearest pub, I found I could not stop, and Martin was laughing so much that others listened in. I ended up standing on a table in a bar in the City being more and more outrageously boringly Randy. The next day I had a vague recollection of the owner asking me to go to the other pub he owned for their New Year's Eve Cabaret, and since I hadn't anything better on offer I went and did the act again.

And so the first of my characters was born. Since I have always been a reasonable mimic, and since I love talking, it wasn't difficult to develop monologues. I gave up Randy, the American banker, when Harry Enfield came along with Loadsamoney, because Randy was not nearly as funny. By that time I had found that I was more comfortable in a woman's character anyway and I had created Serena, the vacuous newscaster who spoke mainly in headlines, Wendy Wilberforce, the Tory local councillor (researched in Pinner at a coffee morning given by Reg and my mother), and various others. I had been trying all week to concoct a theatrical darling, but Agatha was too individual to typecast and, as her client list was mainly male, I hadn't run into many other women.

Stephanie, who was to become Nancy New Age, was telling me about a weekend course she had been on called 'The Pulse'. It had cost almost £2,000 and was, she said, the best money she had ever spent.

'"The Pulse",' I asked, 'is that animal or vegetable?'

'What do you mean?' she replied defensively.

33

'Oh, you know, I mean are we talking throb or bean?'

For a moment Stephanie looked very hurt, as if I wasn't taking her sufficiently seriously, so I asked her to describe it, and she became rather coy, as if I was trying to get a freebie enlightenment. I assured her that it wasn't at all the sort of thing I would want to do.

'How can you know that, without participating?' she said.

'Well –'

'Exactly,' she interrupted. 'I never said this to you before, Sophie, but you are very judgemental. I wonder if that's something to do with your lonely childhood. You had to impose order on the world because you felt so alienated. It must have been difficult to be abandoned, I realize that, but I think you have never really acknowledged your grief.'

'Hold on. I wasn't abandoned. My parents separated. That's not very unusual these days.'

'But not to have known your father.'

'I did know my father. Quite frankly, we were much happier, in my recollection, when he left.' That wasn't quite true, but I suddenly felt very protective towards Reg. 'Anyway, I had a very happy upbringing.'

'That's not quite how I remember it,' she said, all-knowingly.

'Well, it wasn't your childhood,' I said, as patiently as I could.

'But you told me that you were devastated when they sent you away to boarding school.'

I vaguely remembered such a conversation years ago when I had been trying to argue the benefits of the state school system. I had been unhappy at my private school, but after a term my mother had seen this and brought

34

me back to the local comprehensive. She and Reg had been trying to do only what they thought best. I realized that it wasn't worth arguing with Stephanie. Whatever I said in my defence would somehow be worked round to prove her thesis. Whatever her thesis might be. It seemed to be a combination of Freud and massive rationalization. I switched the conversation back to her, a subject she seemed happy to talk about *ad infinitum*. I learned that during 'The Pulse' one was humiliated for several hours, forbidden to go to the toilet, shouted at, forced to express one's worst fantasies and generally reduced to a level of self-loathing one wouldn't have believed possible, then suddenly hugged and reassured until one realized what a wonderful person one was.

'But surely nobody is a wonderful person? We all have our faults. It's no good smiling a beatific smile and insisting that everyone is wonderful underneath. People aren't like that,' I said.

'But that's exactly why you need to do "The Pulse", Sophie, don't you see? You hate yourself and it makes you cynical.'

'I don't hate myself. How many times do I have to tell you?' My voice was rising.

'That's right –' a proselytizing gleam was in her eye – 'be angry, let it all come out.'

'Stephanie,' I said, very calmly.

'Yes?'

'You know those assertiveness courses you were telling me about earlier?'

'Yes. They were good, you know, but not as fundamental as "The Pulse".'

'Stephanie,' I said.

'Yeah?' She was by now, I think, anticipating a new recruit.

35

'As they would say on those courses, just shut up and fuck off!'

To give her her due, she laughed. But then began again.

'You see, Soph, you've just unwittingly hit on one of my problems. I think I take it all a bit too seriously . . .'

'Maybe life doesn't have to be about problems.' I found I was slipping into the role of shrink myself. 'Maybe it's normal to have problems, and abnormal if we don't.'

'If only it were that simple,' she said.

'But it is. It is,' I replied, and gave her a kiss as she left.

7

Apparently, everyone in the audience had suffered some-body like Nancy New Age and I was delighted by the number of laughs she got. I did my half-hour slot, picked up my £10 cash and went out to the front bar to see if there was anyone I knew. There were a couple of people from Edinburgh and we chatted for a while. They said nice things about the act and made some constructive criticism, but then we were joined by some mime artists I didn't know and I began to feel rather excluded from the conversation. That's the trouble with being a bit of a dilettante in the world of theatre. If you don't take it too seriously people don't like having you around much. I suppose it is the same in any profession, but it seems more odd amongst people who spend their lives trying to make other people laugh. Comedy is a very serious business.

I went to the bar to get a round. It was very busy and everyone around me seemed to be very tall. I kept waving my £10 note in the air, but since the bartender couldn't see who the money was attached to, he served others first. I was beginning to get quite bad-tempered when a familiar voice behind me said, with irony, 'Great performance, Miss Fitt.'

I turned and looked up. Greg's face was laughing down at me.

'Here, let me help you.' He attracted the bartender's attention and got in the round. We carried the drinks

37

back to my table and I started to introduce him, but nobody seemed very interested and they had let somebody else take my seat.

'I was sitting over there.' Greg pointed to a table at the back of the pub and we pushed our way over to it.

'Is your name really Miss Fitt,' he asked, 'or is that just because of the act?'

'You mean like Miss Demeanour, or something?'

'Exactly.'

'Would that I were that imaginative,' I said. 'Unfortunately my name really is Sophie Fitt. I hadn't realized how silly it sounded until I grew up and people started calling me Miss Fitt at work. I tried to insist on Ms, but it's awkward, isn't it? I long to get married so that I can change it.'

He looked astonished.

'That was a joke,' I said.

'You're a wicked woman.'

'Am I?' I asked coquettishly. 'What makes you say that?'

'I saw your act. It was good, yes, pretty funny, but ouch! I wouldn't want to be one of your friends.'

'The characters I do aren't my friends,' I said, rather put out. 'They're made up. You know, fictions.'

'Really?'

'Well . . .' I felt a twinge of guilt about Stephanie. 'Anyway, you needn't worry, I don't do men.'

He laughed. 'So I'm safe?'

'Quite safe with me,' I said.

It was odd, but on the two brief occasions I had met him, Greg and I seemed to have fallen quite naturally into flirting. It was as if we had known each other for much longer than we had. I felt quite comfortable in his presence, which I wasn't used to with men I fancied.

And I fancied him rotten. He was wearing black jeans and a black V-necked sweater. What I could see of his chest was quite hairless and boyish, but there was something extremely male about him. I wondered whether he might possibly fancy me too or whether it was just a coincidence that he had turned up at the pub.

'This is my local,' he said, putting an end to my speculations. 'I've been in here a few times, but this is the first time I've talked to anyone. London is a very unfriendly place.'

'And Dublin?' I asked.

'Well,' he said, 'Dublin is a bit too friendly, I suppose.'

I asked him what he meant and he described the scene there. He was a great raconteur and a fervent republican and his comparisons between the British and the Irish made England seem a very dull place. He said that Dublin was a city encapsulating all the benefits and disadvantages of intimacy – the closeness and acceptance, but also the lack of privacy. He liked London because he could be anonymous here.

'But you would prefer it if your local pub were a bit more friendly?' I asked.

'Yes,' he said. 'But now I've met you here, so why am I complaining?'

We ended up in bed. I'm not quite sure how. At no point did either of us make an advance to the other, as such. We stayed in the pub until it closed and then went to Pizza Express. I had asked the waitress to bring some chilli peppers to crumble on to my American Hot. Later on I must have rubbed my eyes because suddenly, in the middle of quite a serious conversation about Joyce, I started screaming. My eyes were running and I thought I had been struck down by a freak blindness. It was

Greg who realized what the problem was, and he accompanied me most solicitously to the Ladies' toilets and plunged my face into a basinful of cold water. That alleviated the problem, but I was still crying involuntarily as I hailed a taxi and Greg decided that he couldn't leave me like that and came back to my flat.

We drank the remains of the Rioja together and fell asleep on the sofa until the early hours, when we both woke up and went, fully clothed, to my big double bed. In the morning I found myself being caressed and gradually undressed. I reciprocated. He was a beautiful, languid lover. When I close my eyes I can still see his face above me and feel the touch of his curls flopping against my skin.

Later, we went for brunch in Hampstead and read the papers. We talked about the latest reviews and what was in the news but not about what had happened. Then he disappeared down the Underground and I window-shopped in Nicole Farhi and walked home. I tried to work out how I felt. It was a combination of exhaustion and elation.

That evening he rang and told me how good he felt. He said he would call again soon. I tried not to feel hurt that he hadn't suggested another meeting. He was obviously keen or he wouldn't have rung in the first place, would he? Or perhaps Irishmen had different rules about these things.

My normal experience of one-night stands is that men always say they will ring and rarely do, which is why I gave them up (until Greg). Once you know the four rules –

1. Nobody ever loses your telephone number.
2. There is not a hope that your phone is out of order

because your mother got through perfectly easily.
3. He didn't try phoning when your mother was on the phone and give up because it was engaged.
4. Yes, you're a feminist and there is no reason at all why you can't ring him; except that if you do your chances of seeing him again go down to about 1 per cent because he'll feel pressured.

then the brief pleasures, if you're lucky, of the act are far outweighed by the insecurities of the next few weeks. On balance it is just not worth it.

So why, I asked myself, did I have to break my resolve with a man who was so good at it that whenever I thought about him my knickers grew moist and I couldn't stop myself smiling in an inanely smug way?

8

'Oh, I shouldn't laugh. It's pathetic really!' Hoots of laughter were coming from Agatha's office when I arrived on Monday.

I peeped round her door to see her lying back in her chair, her legs thrown across the desk and the phone clamped between her cheek and shoulder.

'Yes, all right, darling,' she said to the person on the other end of the phone. 'I won't be cruel. See you soon, darling? I'll call you.' She put down the phone and smiled quite wickedly.

'When my sister and I were young,' she said, in explanation, 'we used to amuse ourselves by playing a game called What If? Let me give you an example. What if Romeo had received Juliet's letter? Shakespeare is full of them. So is Hardy. The whole plot creaks on the fact that somebody missed the post. You can extend it to most of the great plots in literature. We used to while away many an hour with it.'

'Like, what if Jocasta had had a headache?' I said.

'Exactly. Bang goes the greatest tragedy, and Freud along with it.'

'So?' I was enjoying her mirth and the plots that were rapidly dwindling into farce in my mind.

'Well, I think she must have been playing that game with her no-talent husband, because a mutual friend tells me that he is trying to sell a contemporary version of *Othello* where they all live happily ever after. Apparently the Moor knocks her around a bit then sees the error of his ways . . . Oh, dear.'

'What's his name?'

'Oh, I don't know, probably Winston, or something.'

'No, I meant the playwright.'

'My brother-in-law, you mean?' She raised her eyebrows. 'He's called Jack Burton. He used to be quite good, when he was an angry young man, but now he's a middle-aged man who's just rather cross about everything. Probably can't get it up. He wrote one brilliant play called *The Hairs in the Sink*, which I represented –'

For some reason the title was familiar to me, although I couldn't remember having seen the play.

'Was it made into a film?' I asked, wondering if that was where I recognized it from.

'Surprisingly it wasn't,' Agatha replied. 'It was all the rage for a moment or two, but it dated rather more than *Look Back in Anger* and all those others. And, since then, zilch. He went back to teaching. I suspect his pupils thought his work was marvellous, because it really is teenage stuff. Anyway, they threw him out because of his drinking and he's been trying to hawk his work around recently. I do wonder how Dorothy puts up with it.'

'Does she represent him now?'

'What? No, he represents himself now, inasmuch as there's anything to represent. After we parted, no other agent would touch him, frankly –'

'But what about Dorothy?' I asked.

'Dorothy?' she said, as if the name were suddenly unfamiliar.

'I thought that she was an agent . . .' I faltered. Obviously I had misunderstood the story that Janet had told me. Agatha looked almost insulted at the suggestion.

'Wasn't she the other Brown, in Brown and Brown?' I continued rather disingenuously.

'Well, she was. But she was never an agent. Far too lightweight and silly. She barely had the nous to be a secretary – Oh, sorry, darling, I didn't mean – I mean, you're not really a secretary after all.'

It seemed pointless to explain that the look of surprise which had crossed my face was due not to any unintentional insult to my status as secretary, but to the dismissive way in which Agatha had just spoken of her sister.

'Now, where were we?' asked Agatha with a finality that closed the subject.

We began to go through the post. There were some complicated contracts relating to the transfer of a West End musical to Broadway and several large cheques from advertising agencies which made Agatha sigh.

'Just look at this,' she said. 'Richard David has made more money from doing a voice-over for an after-dinner mint ad than he has on the stage for the last ten years. He's a quite wonderful actor – have you ever seen him? No, I suppose a little before your time, but not in fashion.' She rattled on, partly to herself and partly, I felt, to amuse me.

I reached across her desk, took a handful of envelopes out of her in-tray and began opening them and passing back to Agatha the material I couldn't deal with myself. One of the larger envelopes looked as if it had been hand-delivered. The paper was creamy and thick and I thought it would contain an invitation printed on similarly creamy card. But inside was a carefully folded piece of matching notepaper with one sentence typed on it. It read simply, 'YOUR PAST MISTAKES WILL HAUNT YOU.'

I thought it must be some gimmick or other for advertising a play and passed it over the desk to Agatha with a smile.

She looked at it for a few moments. Then she said sarcastically, 'How very profound. Obviously the epigrammatic mind of a great artist is at work again. I don't think we need bother with a response.'

She balled up the paper and threw it at her rubbish bin, shouting 'Goal!' as it reached its target, then grabbed the next item I was holding out to her and, after a quick glance, exclaimed, 'Oh, my God! Sophie, we really are witnessing the death of culture this morning. Even the bloody melodramas can't remain untouched. Just look at this. "Wolf Productions is pleased to announce *Rebecca* by Daphne du Maurier." Do you think it can have escaped their attention that there is already a film of *Rebecca*? Do they really feel they can better Olivier? The next thing they'll try is a remake of *Wuthering Heights* . . . It'll never work. Tens of millions down the drain. We must think of actors for it.'

I looked surprised.

'Second rule of agency, Sophie, get your clients work. We may turn up our classical noses at these philistines from Hollywood, but we do like their money, yes?'

I nodded. 'What's the first rule of agency, then?' I wondered out loud.

'Don't fuck your clients,' said Agatha.

I started with surprise. But it was clear from her face that she didn't know I just had twenty-four hours ago.

'Conflict of interest, causes untold problems, darling.'

If I have one lasting memory of Agatha it is of her that day, her long, slightly veiny legs clad in purple leggings thrown over her desk, Cuban-heeled ankle boots resting next to the phone, her body, slender inside a huge,

45

brightly coloured Latin-American tunic, shaking with laughter. Her leathery, intelligent face looked positively girlish as she leafed through the heap of documents trying to decide which to attend to first.

The only moment when her good humour failed momentarily was when she lighted on a chain letter that urged the recipient to make twelve copies and send them on to friends.

'I'm sure these things are nothing but a conspiracy on the part of manufacturers of photocopiers. Why on earth should I waste your time and my money sending this nonsense on to anybody? Ah, I see, it says that if I don't I shall have bad luck. How mean. Now, which of my acquaintances do you think could have sent me this? Obviously not someone who likes me, because anyone who knew the first thing about me would know I have no intention of doing as instructed. If I knew who it was I would send the bloody thing back to them, bad luck and all!'

I came to enjoy work in the next weeks much more than I had bargained for. Agatha was marvellous company and, although I could see that she would be a fearsome adversary, she was always charming to me in the short periods of time we spent together, sometimes even asking my advice about casting, or other matters on which I might have an informed opinion. After she realized that she could rely on me to take a sensible message, or deal with a crisis without panicking, she began to have longer and longer lunches. This was obviously the part of the day she enjoyed most, and sometimes she would come back to the office full of anecdotes and *bonhomie*, and beckon me into her office to regale me with the latest gossip.

I was so happy doing my job that it almost worried me. I kept telling myself that it was only a temporary job, that the wages were pitiful and there was no hope of promotion in such a small office, but the more time passed, the more involved I became. There was a minor set-back to my good spirits when Greg rang me to say that he had to go back to Dublin for a couple of weeks. He was very friendly and promised to call as soon as he was back, but I was slightly put out that, having talked to me for five minutes, he then asked to be put through to Agatha, which made me feel like a switchboard. That afternoon Agatha gave me a ticket for a first night at the Bush for which she was double-booked and I went, and even got myself invited to the party. I must have acquitted myself reasonably well, because after that Agatha regularly asked me to go to plays and film previews on her behalf. I began to feel more like her protégée than her secretary. A fact that did not go unnoticed in the office.

As I'd worked for five years in a bank, the paperwork was quite straightforward for me. I decided after a couple of weeks that the systems Agatha used were ludicrously wasteful of time and space and I asked if she had ever thought about computerizing the files. Agatha's rather laid-back manner belied a keen business mind and she sat up and listened as soon as she heard the word cost-cutting. Life would have been a lot easier, however, if I had discussed my plans with Janet and Anthony White first.

Janet did not like the fact that Agatha treated me more as a friend than a secretary whilst ignoring her completely. I could understand her point of view, especially since Agatha, if she addressed her at all, always managed to get her name wrong. Although she was only in her thirties, Janet was an old-style secretary who had studied at Pitman's and preferred shorthand to dicta-phones. Her almost subservient manner seemed to suit Anthony's ego very well, but clearly Agatha despised it. I often wondered how someone as classy as Agatha had ended up with a partner like Anthony, who was so very obviously inferior, but it was a combination that seemed to work quite well and Agatha would always speak to Anthony with respect. Whenever there was a problem with accounts or VAT, Agatha would wave me over to Anthony to sort it out. She behaved as if details like figures were too boring for her to attend to. This was an act, and one she used to great effect when negotiating, tricking the person on the other end of the phone into believing that she wasn't really on the ball and then slicing in with amazingly accurate-sounding arithmetic as soon as she had them off-balance. She wasn't above rattling off calculations which, if you thought about them for just a moment, turned out not to add up. In my first week I had pointed this out to her, thinking that she had inadvertently made a mistake.

'Really, darling?' she said ingenuously. 'I hope not to our detriment?'

'No, not at all,' I said, showing her the piece of paper on which I had worked out the sums and then discover-ing, as I looked up at her grinning face, that I had been as fooled as the producer she was talking to.

'So irresponsible of them not to check, don't you think?' She laughed.

When it came to the rigorous keeping of financial records, however, Agatha really couldn't be bothered. Her fun was in the deal. Once the money was in the bank gaining interest, she became bored. Anthony was therefore invaluable to her.

I couldn't understand why he, who had all the accounts on computer after all, should so object to my idea of buying another couple of terminals and enlarging the capacity to take the day-to-day information, as well as giving us a word-processing facility. Perhaps it was simply because the suggestion had come from me and not him, or because of pressure from Janet, who had decided irrationally that it would mean more work. We compromised. A separate computer was installed for me and I arranged for a software consultant to come in and be briefed by me about the system I wanted. Janet continued as before, muttering about the trouble there would be when Viv returned. Much to my astonishment, Agatha requested a screen in her office and asked me to show her how to use it. I put on all the addresses and telephone numbers and taught her how to look them up, and became used to hearing her squeal with joy as the information she wanted appeared on the screen. She even ceremoniously threw away the dog-eared Rotodex that sat on her desk.

I set about gradually transferring the salient details of the clients' contracts to the hard disk whenever I had spare moments. It was a task that demanded a great deal of concentration, and there were times when I regretted suggesting the computer at all, especially since, as a temp, I wouldn't experience any of the long-term benefits, but I hate not being occupied and I was fascinated by the idea of cataloguing the important moments of each client's life since the late 1950s.

I had just finished putting on all the contracts of the clients whose name began with A when Agatha fell ill and was away from the office.

9

Hallowe'en is Martin's birthday, although he is the least spooky of people. We were meant to be having dim sum together at lunch because, he told me, he had an important date that evening, but in the end he cancelled lunch and made it dinner because the air hostess got cold feet, pleading a late flight from Las Palmas.

Martin is a great person to eat Chinese food with because, like me, he understands the principle that you order everything you could possibly eat on the menu and worry about the bill later.

We were on our second portion of pancakes for the crispy aromatic duck (why do they only ever give you two each?) when he remarked, 'Soph, you seem a bit down in the mouth. What's up?'

I wiped a spot of hoisin sauce from my chin and began to tell him. Agatha was ill and her clients did not like it. I was a genial enough person to chat with while she was on the phone or out at lunch, but really I was only a message-bearer. They expected her in the office during office hours, at least, and far from expressing sympathy when they heard she was unable to talk to them because she had severe flu, some of them became shirty and impatient. I felt utterly inadequate at dealing with them. Also there was the problem of Janet and Anthony, who had been unhelpful to the point of being obstructive. I had been trying to sort out as many of the problems as I could on Agatha's behalf, so that when she returned things would not have piled up too much, but whenever I asked for Anthony's advice, however humbly, he always made some excuse. It had been a horribly frustrating couple of days.

'Do you know,' said Martin, 'you're doing exactly what you did at the bank. You're such a perfectionist. For God's sake, Soph, you're a temporary secretary. When you first got this job you were talking about how much you were enjoying not having any responsibility. Only a month or so later you're taking the whole agency on your shoulders. No wonder this bloke White resents you. It must be bad enough for him to work with one strong woman, let alone two! He sounds a bit of a wimp.'

'He's not really. He has a filthy temper. Though, now you mention it, he probably does have a bit of a penis problem.'

'What?' Martin looked up from rolling his pancake.

'Well, he's got this ridiculous sports car –'

'Oh, honestly, Soph.'

'Jerry had a Lamborghini,' I said, pursuing my argument.

'Jerry's an arsehole, but he doesn't seem to have much of a problem with his dick.'

'This conversation is getting too scatological for me,' I said primly.

Martin laughed. 'That's rich, from you ... Look, if there are things you can't cope with, why don't you ring Agatha tomorrow and take some of the work round and sort it out?'

'I don't want to bother her, though. She sounded absolutely awful today.'

'Sophie, it is her agency.'

'As she herself reminds everyone.' I laughed.

'Exactly. Now, more importantly, where's the squid with chilli and salt?'

As he asked the question a waiter appeared with a trolley of the dishes we had ordered. It looked rather a lot, even for us, but we ate valiantly for a couple of hours. One of the great myths about Chinese food is that it makes you feel very full when you are eating it and hungry an hour afterwards. I have never found this to be the case. While I was eating I thought I could go on for ever, but I felt so very full after we had paid the bill that I suggested going for a walk to aid digestion. Martin was wavering. I remembered that he was still having to get up at six in the morning to go to work, but I reminded him that it was his birthday and, besides, if he went home straight away he would be besieged by unpleasant children shouting Trick or Treat into his entryphone.

We walked all the way to Westminster Bridge, chatting. I had been so immersed in work recently that I had hardly talked to anyone outside the world of stage and screen. Martin quite likes opera, but that is about as far as his interest in the arts goes. It was refreshing to talk about other things. It was one of those typically London cold, slightly foggy nights, and we walked along arm in arm to keep warm. The streetlights along Whitehall were surrounded by haloes of ochre mist and the air smelt autumnal, like leaves beginning to rot.

He told me that he had begun taking Spanish lessons at night school and was enjoying it. This seemed an extraordinary thing for someone as highly qualified as him to be doing. He explained that he had never really learned to speak a foreign language and, anyway, he wanted to travel. I told him he sounded like a Miss World contestant. He told me that I had a particularly unpleasant suburban snobbery about me at times. I told him he was becoming boringly European, and we generally got along very well.

As he hailed a taxi in Parliament Square, he said, 'Well, this should get you home before the witching hour. Isn't there some superstition about looking in the mirror on Hallowe'en and seeing the man you are going to marry?'

'Where on earth did you hear that?' I asked.

'Well, from Darryl, as a matter of fact,' he said rather bashfully.

That was another thing I intensely disliked about the air hostess. I felt sure that Darryl was an invented name, and somehow it was just as bad if it wasn't.

'Oh no, Martin, you're not thinking of breaking in and stealing up behind her while she's taking off her make-up?'

'Actually I have a key,' he said, and then added, when I looked surprised, 'so that I can water her plants when she is away.'

'Martin, you're a complete imbecile! I thought I had spent the evening talking to a grown-up person, but I find I was wrong. You're a teenage romantic!'

'And I love you too,' he said, good-humouredly, and slammed the cab door.

I was home by midnight, and I'm ashamed to admit that I did light a candle and stand in front of my cheval mirror hopefully for a few seconds, but my would-be vision was interrupted by the phone ringing.

'Hi, you.'

'Who is this?'

'Woah, short memory, Miss Fitt.'

'Greg? How are you? Where are you? Still in Dublin.

Right.' Why on earth was he ringing at this time of night? I hadn't heard from him since he left, weeks ago.

'I was just thinking about you.' He made those simple words sound incredibly suggestive. 'I'm getting the afternoon flight back. Can we meet tomorrow?'

I said fine and we arranged to meet in a bar in Camden. When I put the phone down I was trembling. I hoped I hadn't sounded too off-hand and reran the conversation in my head several times, squirming at the bit where I didn't recognize his voice. Still, I told myself, better not to look too keen. Then I told myself not to be so silly. We were far too mature to play cat and mouse games. Then I thought about what to wear and remembered that all my good underwear was in a service-wash downstairs. Then I had a drink and told myself that I really wasn't very excited at all. Then I stripped the bed and ironed some crisp white broderie anglaise sheets that my mother, in a rare display of good taste, had given me for my birthday. I never iron. Then it took me hours to get to sleep.

'Garlic!' rasped Agatha as she opened the door, reeling slightly. 'Don't worry, it is supposed to be good for colds. What was it, Indian?'

'Chinese,' I replied, rather embarrassed.

'I've never much cared for Chinese, although I suspect that it has changed since I last tasted it. I always found it rather bland.'

I supplied her with a brief description of the night before's menu and she looked surprised.

'In my day,' she said, 'it was nothing but that terrible fluorescent red sauce.'

'Sweet and sour?'

'That's the one. I always found it very sweet and not at all sour.'

I assured her that recently the fashion seemed to be for Peking or Szechuan cuisine rather than Cantonese.

'When I'm better, you must recommend a restaurant,' she whispered.

I felt rather awkward talking about such trivia when she was obviously finding it difficult to speak.

'Now come and sit down. I shall recline. This bloody flu is making me desperately lethargic. Here is a set of keys, in case you come again. I really can't be doing with all this getting up and down for visitors.'

She did not look well. Her hair, unwashed for several days, hung in greasy rat's-tails around her face. Her complexion was sallower than usual and I noticed, as she showed me into what she called her day room, that her walk was weary. She was wearing a Japanese silk kimono which gaped and revealed a distinctly old neck. She lay down on a *chaise-longue* that was upholstered in gold velvet, threw a dirty looking tartan rug across her legs and started coughing chestily. I had bought her some yellow chrysanthemums, which she looked at despondently.

'In most countries, they signify death,' she said. 'Go and find a vase in the kitchen.'

The flat consisted of four rooms leading off a rather claustrophobic corridor. The day room was decorated in much the same style as her office – all the walls covered with memorabilia and striking abstract paintings, the furniture a mixture of Victorian and contemporary. It would have been very dark had not the fourth wall been entirely window, opening on to a balcony with railings that looked over a spectacular view of Hampstead Heath. The kitchen was at the far end of the corridor. I supposed that the mansion block in which Agatha lived had been built in the 1930s or thereabouts. The kitchen had not been refurbished. It was shockingly shabby, with old-fashioned wooden cupboards with peeling light-green paint. The only concession to the second half of the century was a white microwave which stood as alien as a spaceship on the zinc surround to the sink. It was the kitchen of someone who had no concept of home. I found an old wine carafe for the flowers.

'How churlish I am, darling,' she said, as I reappeared. 'The flowers are lovely and I am being morbid. I feel so ghastly. Do forgive me.'

'Have you seen a doctor?' I inquired, as she began to cough again.

'I've consulted my dietitian. I loathe doctors,' she replied.

'But perhaps you should be taking something?'

'I don't take drugs. They harm the body's immune system. I never get ill, but when I do, it is because the body is trying to cleanse itself. Nothing religious, so don't look at me so sceptically. It's natural.'

Although this would have sounded barmy to most people, it struck some distant chord in my mind.

'I think my father believed something similar,' I said. It was a fetish, like the health food that my mother had never been able to understand.

'Well, then . . . Now let's get on with business, before I get too tired.'

I started to explain the various problems I was having. Paul Montefiore, who was an actor I disliked intensely, mostly because he always seemed to play villains in gratuitously violent films, but also because he treated me like a dumb blonde on the phone and addressed me as 'love', was demanding that his contract for the television series he was working on be renegotiated. The producers were very willing to renegotiate, but only as long as his fee went down, and otherwise they were saying they would sack him. He was apparently as obnoxious on the set as he was in real life.

'Oh, dear,' said Agatha, 'well, we can't tell him that, can we? I think we had better call their bluff. The series is far too far along for them to scrap him. And he does, incomprehensibly, have quite a little following of bully boys and masochistic housewives. Just tell them that he's no longer requesting a rise and tell him they won't budge. Can you manage that?'

I said I thought I could, although I didn't relish the prospect.

'All part of the job,' she said. 'Oh, hallo, darling. Here, come and sit with me,' she added for the benefit of her cat, who had just wandered into the room.

I thought, but didn't say, that it was all part of her job, and she earned a great deal more than me. I felt, not for the first time that week, that Agatha was exploiting my good nature and my competence, but her breathing was so laboured that I didn't want to upset her further. I decided to ask for a rise once she came back to the office.

'Next!' she said wearily.

'Well, Cormac O'Hara's play is due to start previewing on Broadway next week and they still haven't signed the contract.'

'What?'

'I've chased and chased, but they keep saying that it is in the pipeline.'

'Tell them I don't care where it is as long as it turns up on my desk, signed, by close of business tomorrow. Otherwise we injunct. If you can't tell them then send a fax. Or do both. Ring, and then confirm by fax. We have to be tough on this one. Cormac is so mild-mannered he would let them get away with murder.'

Even though she was really very poorly, Agatha became quite animated when crusading on behalf of her favourite clients and Cormac O'Hara, a gentle Irish playwright whose most recent play had broken through and had been running in the West End for over a year, was certainly one of those. I adored watching her when she was in this kind of mood and wondered if she had been born as confident, or if it was something she had learned. I took down an outraged Agatha fax and turned to the next item.

'There's another letter from the drama department of

a university in California, asking permission to put on *The Hairs in the Sink* in their season of "Seminal Works of the 1960s", they call it.' I had remembered, when I opened the air-mail envelope, that a similar letter had arrived on my first day at the office, but I hadn't known then who the author was. I had put it in the pile of post in Agatha's in-tray and hadn't seen it since.

'Oh, give that here. Seminal, indeed! I'll deal with it. Is that all?' she asked.

'Well, nearly –'

'Wait a minute,' she interrupted. 'You're not related to the artist Marcus Fitt, are you?'

I hesitated, wondering whether I had heard her correctly.

'Yes, as a matter of fact I'm his daughter.'

'Well, well,' she said. 'You see I've been thinking about what you said about your father being interested in naturopathy and remembering that the only person I have ever encountered who really sympathized with my view was Marcus. I've been trying to place his name for the last half-hour, while we've been talking, but my brain's addled with this flu. Then I realized it was Fitt, just like yours. How is he? The old scoundrel.'

'I really have no idea,' I said. It sounded ungracious, but it was the truth.

'No idea? He's not dead, is he?'

'Not as far as I'm aware, but I haven't seen him for over twenty years and he gave up sending postcards when I was about ten.'

Agatha seemed not in the least perturbed by this news. Nor did her face fill with a kind of plastic sympathy, as most people's do when they hear that I never see him. I am so sick of that look, which always reminds me of Mrs Thatcher's 'concerned' face, that I very rarely mention my father or his absconding to anyone.

'Unreliable as ever! Goodness, it must be a good twenty-five years since I saw him last. He was a most attractive man. Most attractive. Completely irresponsible, but so very attractive. Not, I think, a first-rate artist, and certainly not a first-rate person, but brilliant company. A whole group of us once spent a weekend on a kind of prototype health farm eating carrots. Oh, we laughed, God, how we laughed.'

As she recounted her memories, stroking the cat steadily and rhythmically, I sat rapt in the darkening room. I did not remember my father as an attractive man, although in photographs he certainly looked handsome. I always found his presence rather overbearing. He was a big man, who seemed to fill a room, and I remember him smelling of French tobacco. Most of all I remember his temper, which did not flare up often but was always somehow lurking around him. He was not a violent man physically, but there was threat of cruelty about him. I was certain that I had never seen him laugh.

'Marcus was a brilliant raconteur. He never let a lie stand in the way of a good story. In those days we used to hang around in coffee bars in the King's Road, and Soho. We didn't really drink then, or take drugs much – a lot of that 1960s stuff is such a myth, you know – but we would be up until all hours talking, and fucking of course.'

Agatha seemed to have brightened up enormously recalling these events. It was so dark now that I couldn't see her face, but I could hear the smile on it. There were lots of questions that I wanted to ask her, not least whether she had fucked my father, but Agatha's mind was very butterfly-like and I had found before that to interrupt was often to change the subject.

'Those were golden times, You just can't imagine, Sophie. I'm almost embarrassed to think how idealistic we were. Dorothy and I of course were terribly close then, virtually inseparable, and there were a couple of jazz guitarists, can't remember their names, and Jack, of course. We all went on Aldermaston marches together. Marcus was always late, always with another woman, always cadging a couple of quid, and never, as I recall, paying it back. But never mind. He was good value.' She rambled on and on. Weekends spent in Walberswick. I had seen some of the paintings of beach scenes from that period in an exhibition once. Holidays in Cornwall, where apparently he had insisted on buying crabs and boiling them up alive until they screamed. It seemed as though the fluctuating group of friends had been very close for some considerable period of time.

'Whatever happened to him?' Agatha suddenly asked herself, as if she had forgotten that he had anything to do with me. 'No, I remember, he had a grand passion for a little waitress who none of us found remotely interesting. We just couldn't see it at all. When she entered a room, somehow the conversation simply stopped. And then we just drifted apart, I suppose, as people do . . . I think I remember that he got married. I remember thinking that very odd indeed –'

I felt bound to interrupt at this point. Somehow the vision of my mother surrounded by the motley crew of bohemian intellectuals Agatha had described had brought tears to my eyes. I have often found that educated middle-class people who profess socialist principles are at their most intolerant whenever they encounter people they consider inferior.

'The waitress was, I believe, my mother,' I said defensively.

'I suppose that was the reason then.'

'For him getting married? No, I don't think it was a shotgun wedding, if that's what you mean. I think that initially my father was very much in love.'

'No, no, no. You misunderstand me, darling, I meant that that was the reason we didn't see him any more. He had you to bring up.' That sounded a bit false to me, but I was pleased Agatha had made the effort to redeem what was becoming an uncomfortable conversation.

'Of course, you don't look like him at all. But I think you have inherited something. Both very charming, of course, and sharp. Sharpness. Yes, you are both very sharp.'

It was a double-edged observation, which I decided to take as a compliment. I tried to get her to say more about those days, but I think she was wary, having obviously touched a nerve with me.

I got up and switched on the light. I gave her some letters I had typed that needed her signature, and she signed with one hand, shading her eyes from the light with the other.

'Marvellous, darling. Now, will you have a drink?'

I said I would love one.

'Well, you'll have to get a glass from the kitchen. Squeeze a couple of lemons, would you, and bring in the honey.'

I did as I was told. I found the lemon squeezer in the sink under several saucepans which looked as if they had been left to soak for some days. The honey was on the draining board, its top off and a teaspoon standing in it.

'There's ice in the fridge!' Agatha called out.

There certainly was. Most of the fridge was ice, because

it had obviously never been defrosted. There were a few opened tins of soup languishing in the fridge part and an ice tray stuck in the freezer. I hacked it out with a blunt knife and brought everything I had collected in to Agatha on the lid of an old square biscuit tin, since I couldn't find a tray.

'Would you be an angel, darling, and boil a kettle for me? And wash out this cup.' She held out a chipped mug. I took it gingerly and washed it out in the kitchen as best I could. There was no sign of any washing-up liquid. I boiled a kettle of water on the ancient gas cooker.

'Now,' she said, as I returned, kettle in one hand and mug in the other, 'in that cupboard you will find some whisky.' She pointed at the small mahogany sideboard next to me. I bent down and opened it. There was a box that had obviously contained twelve bottles of Glenmorangie. The first two divisions were empty and the third contained a half-full bottle. I handed it to Agatha.

'Now would you like it straight, with ice, or my special Hot Toddy Whisky Sour, excellent for colds?'

I don't really care for whisky, but as I wasn't being offered a choice, and a cursory glance in the sideboard had shown that there was nothing else, I asked for a small measure neat. I thought the stale-smelling ice might poison me.

'I don't suppose my nutritionist would approve on an empty stomach,' said Agatha, 'but what the hell!' She sipped the hot cocktail she had mixed and, when it was sufficiently cold, downed it in one and sighed.

'Would you like me to get you some supper?' I volunteered.

'How kind you are,' said Agatha, as if surprised. It seemed a normal sort of offer to me. In any case, I was only thinking of a pizza from the takeaway on South End Green. 'But no thanks. My sister is cooking for me tonight.'

'Dorothy? But I thought . . .'

'Yes, well, we haven't been the best of friends over the years, but there comes a time, doesn't there?'

I nodded, not knowing really what she was talking about, but unwilling to interrupt.

'I wonder if she's aged? She used to be terribly pretty, but it often doesn't last, does it?' She poured herself another drink, using considerably more whisky than hot water and lemon juice, and waved the bottle at me. I looked at my watch. It was nearly seven-thirty and I was meeting Greg at eight. I had no idea it was so late. I explained that I had an appointment and finished my drink very quickly.

Agatha came to the door with me and, to my great surprise, kissed me with some affection on both cheeks.

'Thank you so much for coming, darling. It's been quite a tonic.'

I told her to get better soon because I couldn't stand the atmosphere in the office much longer without her there to alleviate it.

She laughed and told me she would be back in no time.

11

I needn't have taken a taxi back down from Hampstead. I would have had plenty of time to make my own way home, take a long bath and change, because Greg was nearly an hour late. I was quietly fuming by the time he arrived, as I had longed to hear more about Agatha and Dorothy's feud, but his smile was so disarming that I could not be angry for more than a few seconds. What I particularly liked was the way he leaned across the table, knocking over the half-full bottle of Pinot Grigio and my glass with his leather jacket, and, completely undeterred, kissed me luxuriantly on the mouth.

I have had quite a few relationships in my life. In fact, I was quite a raver at Cambridge. Somebody once called me a promiscuous dyed-blonde slut at a party and I was most offended, protesting that my hair colour was natural. My most serious relationship since university was also my biggest mistake. He was my boss after my training year at the bank. And he was married. I didn't know he was married when it started, which really isn't much of an excuse, because it went on for at least a year after I found out. Jerry is American, like most of the bank's employees (that's how he managed to conceal his wife, and, yes, two kids, from me in the first place). She lives in Connecticut and he in New York, London and Connecticut. He was sent to London because he is a tough manager with orders to kick shit out of the British graduate recruits, who were thought by head office in New York, probably justifiably in most cases, to be arrogant and lazy. Only four of the ten people I started with survived the first year. Jerry wasn't able to get to me with his normal techniques because I worked very hard and I made him laugh. I avoided his coruscating criticisms because he thought I was a peculiarly English dippy lady. For some reason I never examine too closely I was attracted to Jerry from the start, although I professed, like everyone else, to hate him. There was something almost clichéd about his good looks and his power. It was as if he had walked into the bank off the set of *LA Law*. He was, to use one of his favourite words, a winner.

The only thing that makes human beings the same as each other is that we always think we are different. If one of my friends had told me she was having an affair with her married boss, I would have told her that these things never ever work. Get out now! I would have said, and indeed, all my friends who knew, and particularly the ones who had met him, said that. But, like many another hapless mistress, I thought that this was special. I suppose that life would be very boring if we all did what was in our best interests. Emma Bovary wouldn't have been quite the same person if she had just been sensible. It horrifies me now that I told myself this was more than an affair. He, of course, did nothing to disabuse me of my romantic notions. When Martin told me recently that Jerry had taken up with a customer of the bank since I left (at least he is keeping it out of the office this time), I said, 'She must be mad!' Martin just looked at me silently. Which is a long way round of saying that since Jerry and I broke up a couple of years ago I haven't had a very high opinion of men, and I haven't trusted anyone, especially myself, enough to become involved.

Which is partly why, I suppose, I was literally quivering when Greg returned from the bar with two glasses, another bottle of wine and a dishcloth.

When he asked me where I would like to have supper, I found myself saying, 'Why don't we go back to my place and order in a pizza?'

He smiled and handed me my coat, and as we walked up Parkway he put his arm round me as if it were the most natural thing in the world, and I felt, for the first time in years, as if I were part of a couple.

I think the pizza-delivery boy must have been quite surprised, because I opened the door wearing only Greg's T-shirt, which was the first thing I could lay my hands on when the door bell rang.

Greg and I had been talking as we walked along Regent's Park Road, but had become silent with a kind of nervous anticipation as we climbed the stairs to my flat, and as soon as I had phoned the pizza place we had fallen upon one another ravenously. We were good in bed together, and on the kitchen floor. By the time we came up for air, the pizza was cold, but it still tasted delicious. I could have been eating cold fried eggs and felt the same. I was really happy.

'May I stay the night?'

Everything about this man was wonderful. I thought of the tirade against 'new men' that I was working on for my comedy act and felt rather chastened. Here was a man who had genuine courtesy and respect for other people. It was something precious and I shouldn't mock it.

'Of course. Do you want to have a bath?'

'I'd love to.'

'The only thing is, I have to warn you, my bathroom décor is awful and it wasn't my choice . . .'

He laughed. 'I'm really not interested in things like that.'

Nevertheless, I lit a candle so that the avocado bathroom suite wouldn't be too glaringly off-putting. We lay for a long time in the warm scented water. I've always thought that bathing together is almost more intimate than sex. My only physical complaint about Jerry was that he was obsessed with showers and the inadequate water pressure in London, compared to the States. Whenever I tried to entice him into my bath he would pull a face and say, 'Why would anyone want to hang around in dirty water?'

Greg is one of those people who seem equally relaxed talking or being silent. When there were pauses in the conversation I didn't feel the need to fill the spaces by chatting or making brittle jokes, as I normally do. He talked a little about his family. He is the youngest of eight children. He said that when they were small all the children, none of whom was separated by more than two years in age, used to sleep widthways in two double beds. Their bath was in the kitchen with a curtain round it, so for him any bathroom with a door that closed was luxury. He was still close to his five sisters, who had spoiled him like crazy when he was a child, but wasn't really in contact with his two brothers, the oldest in the family, who thought that he had had too easy a time and that it had made him 'soft'. He did an impersonation of them saying, 'Our Greg's an actor now', his face contorted with affectionate disapproval.

My solitary upbringing was so utterly pampered and idyllic in comparison, it sounded almost unreal, like the life of the advert family that I had yearned for as a child. I suspected that he was picturing my mother and myself playing with the washing-up bubbles in our sparkling kitchen and marvelling over the softness of our skin. I thought how much she would approve of Greg and hoped that he would like her too, but not excessively. Then, to counteract the picture of domestic bliss, I mentioned my father.

'I learned more about him today than I have in nearly twenty years!' I said, describing my conversation with Agatha.

'Don't you ever miss him?'

'I suppose I must have done at first. Maybe I just blocked it out. When Agatha was talking about him I did feel a kind of yearning to meet him. I think I would be terrified, though . . .'

'Terrified of what?' Greg moved forward so that small waves of water sloshed up and down the bath. He put his hands on my shoulders and looked into my eyes.

'Oh, that he would be a disappointment. Agatha's very good at enthusing about things, you know – well, of course, you do know. Or maybe that I would be a disappointment to him, that he wouldn't like me . . .'

The sentence hung in the air. Unaccountably I felt tears welling up in my eyes, but I didn't want to raise my hands to wipe them, because I didn't want to move Greg's hands. Suddenly I felt very vulnerable and I looked away.

'Come on,' said Greg. 'Let's wash you.' He soaped me all over like a child, then got out of the bath so that I could lie down and rinse myself. Then he rubbed me down with a towel and, with surprising strength, picked me up and carried me to bed.

We spent hours silently kissing, exploring, licking,

sucking. It was only when he entered me with a sigh of pleasure, opened his eyes, looked down at me and smiled that he said, 'I like you.'

12

The note was typed on familiar-looking vellum and read simply, 'REJECT ME AT YOUR PERIL, BITCH.'

It startled me. I picked the envelope off the top of the wastepaper basket and saw that I shouldn't have opened it anyway, because it was marked 'Personal and Confidential'. The address was typed in full, but there was no stamp. I wondered if it had come in the second post, but then realized it must have been hand-delivered.

I had already rung Agatha once to tell her that the contract for Cormac O'Hara was through and that the money had been wired to the agency's bank account. She was sounding less hoarse and more cheerful. She had decided to indulge herself by taking the rest of the week off, if I felt I could manage. Having assured her I could, I didn't want to ring her again, especially not to read her this. I remembered that the last time a similar note had arrived she had simply thrown it away. I wondered if she knew the sender and what sort of game was being played.

I had come into the office very early. Greg had an audition at nine o'clock and he had to go back to his flat and change. After he left I tried to sleep a little, but I was so wired I couldn't. I had a strong cappuccino in the patisserie downstairs as soon as it opened and arrived at the office feeling light-headed. I was in such a good mood that it must have rubbed off on Janet, who was positively friendly – at least, she said hallo for the first time in days.

I read the note again, and wondered whether I should show it to her, in our new spirit of camaraderie. I wish I had now, because it would have saved a awful lot of misunderstanding. What I did instead was put it under the pile of Agatha's mail on her desk.

The rest of the day was relatively uneventful. I managed to file all the work I had done in Agatha's absence and put the items that required her attention in order of priority on her desk. I started putting the contract details for the authors whose names began with B on to the computer, but found that by the early afternoon my sleepless night was beginning to catch up with me. Anthony White had gone home early – Janet explained that Thursday was his evening with his son, Keith – and I decided that I would too. Janet thought that I should ask Agatha's permission. I was reluctant to do so, since it seemed so demeaning, but in the end I called, not wanting to store up trouble for myself with Anthony White in the morning. Her number was engaged. My tiredness was now making me irritable. I put down the phone and left without further consultation.

I spent Friday loading the Bs on to the computer virtually without interruption. The office was quieter than I had ever known it. When Agatha was around the place buzzed with energy. It was as if she created business by her presence. I found Anthony's fidgetiness wearisome in comparison. He had also developed the annoying habit, in Agatha's absence, of dictating to Janet in our corridor-cum-office, rather than in his own. I decided to take the files into Agatha's office and do the work on her terminal.

The penultimate folder in the B section was labelled Burton. Normally there were two files in each client's folder. One was for the last year's correspondence, which would then be stored at the end of each year in huge metal boxes stacked in the cellar of the building.

A few weeks before, Agatha had asked me to look up a letter of agreement concerning Cormac O'Hara's first play in 1974 which had been mistakenly filed there. It was surprisingly dry in the cellar, but badly lit, with only one light bulb, and I thought I heard the rustle of mice as I stepped gingerly down the wooden staircase from the door in the small lobby. The door closed behind me with a bang that made me jump, but didn't worry me unduly because it was a Yale lock that could be easily opened from the inside. What I found more frightening was the strange, disembodied wailing sound that seemed to be coming from the far corner, until I realized that it was the cook from the Chinese restaurant next door singing over his wok.

The other file contained anything pertaining to contracts. These were not filed annually because they stayed in force throughout the period of copyright, in the case of playwrights, and employment, in the case of actors. I expected Jack Burton's folder to be heavier. There was no correspondence file, which didn't surprise me because he now handled his own work, but there were only two documents in his contracts file, the original agreement for the production of the play and what appeared to be a book contract. I hadn't seen one of these before because most of the As and other Bs were actors, with much more straightforward agreements. I made a note to ask Agatha which details needed recording and started on the next letter of the alphabet.

I stayed late in the office, partly because I had challenged myself to finish the Cs by the end of the week and partly because I had no plans for the evening. Greg had been invited to dinner with the director of the Maguire Seven film and Martin had an unspecified arrangement. He had sounded rather pleased with himself on the phone and when I asked him whether he had bonked the air hostess yet, he replied that he couldn't talk right now. By which I assumed that he had. I imagined him blushing uncomfortably at the other end of the phone, and everyone in the office knowing exactly what he was trying not to talk about, and teasing him.

I caught sight of Stephanie in the cheese queue at Sainsbury's and spent several minutes lurking round bacon and sausages, which I imagined she, as a vegetarian, might avoid. I thought I was safe when I saw her leave the shop, but it turned out that she had forgotten to replenish her supply of mung beans and she joined the quick-check-out queue two behind me. I was surprised at the havoc the five items in my basket were about to wreak on my digestive system if I ate them in the wrong order and declined to join a sponsored meditation the next weekend, although I did offer to contribute 50p an hour.

'It's not timed, Sophie. It's not a kind of endurance test.'

I was just wondering what it was, in that case, and I wasn't quick enough to side-step the dinner invitation for the next week.

I tried to prepare my routine for the pub but found, as I paced round the flat, that I couldn't think of anything but Greg. We were going to have dinner together after my gig the next evening.

74

'Shall we try to eat something other than pizza together?' he had said.

'Do you think this relationship is strong enough to endure an Indian?' I replied.

'I like taking risks.'

So I suggested a restaurant in Westbourne Grove where he had never been.

But that was twenty-four hours away.

If my mother hadn't rung to tell me that she and Reg had seen a bargain in a travel agent's window and decided on the spur of the moment to go for a week's winter break in Madeira, it would have been a very dull evening.

They were leaving the next day and she wanted my advice about what clothes to take. Since I nearly always wear cut-off Levi's and a T-shirt on holiday I wasn't much help, although I did agree that 'something for the evenings' would be advisable in a four-star hotel, knowing very well that my mother never travels without at least three outfits per day in her two vast suitcases. She was in a very chatty mood and told me in enormous detail about Reg's progress with Weightwatchers. It sounded as if she would have little to be ashamed of when he stripped down to his trunks by the lagoon-shaped pool. She must have noticed after about half an hour that I wasn't saying much, because she interrupted herself, mid-brochure, and said, 'How are you getting on, then?'

I had been deliberating whether to tell her about Greg. It seemed a bit soon. I'm rather superstitious about these things so I just said that I had met someone.

'Is he nice?'

'Well, of course he's nice,' I said impatiently. 'He's gorgeous.'

'Looks aren't everything, you know, Sophie.'

For someone who spends at least an hour a day anointing herself with the entire range of Clarins, this was a revelation.

'Well, you should look after your skin too,' she said in her defence.

I changed the subject to work and told her that things had been a bit tough since my boss was ill. Then I remembered the conversation that Agatha and I had been having on Wednesday afternoon.

'Actually, Mum, my boss says she knew you ages ago.'

'Oh, really? What's his name?' My mother gave up taking any interest in my job after my barmy (her word) decision to leave the bank.

'Agatha Brown. She says that she knew my father and that she met you . . .'

I realized that I had encountered a very stony silence on the other end of the phone.

'Yes, well, she would, wouldn't she?'

'Which is to say?'

'Which means that, if you want my opinion, she's a horrible bitch and I wouldn't have a lot to do with her if I were you.'

I couldn't stop myself laughing. It was very rare for my mother to have anything bad to say about anyone. The word bitch cropped up in her vocabulary about as often as the word Cartesian. I was intrigued.

'No, I won't explain, if you don't mind,' she continued. 'Just don't say I didn't warn you.'

I realized that now was not the time to press, so I changed the subject back to sun protection factors, reminded her to take some insect repellent, 'And don't forget the malaria tablets.'

'Are you sure? They never told us that in the travel agent's.'

'Well, they'll say anything, won't they? No, really, Mum, I was joking.'

She tutted and we both put down our receivers with equilibrium restored.

13

'. . . And have you ever wondered what's happened to
language these days? No, I don't mean kids in the street
telling you to fuck off if you don't give them a penny for
the guy. Penny, I say laughingly, whatever happened to
a penny? It's fuck off now if you don't give them a
pound coin. No, I'm not going all Mary Whitehouse on
you, I'm talking about common, everyday language . . .
Yes, sir, that thing that the rest of us can read and
write,' I said to the man at the back, who had been
heckling me all the way through. 'What I mean is,
everything's got a daft name these days . . . British Rail
started it when they realized that they'd be done under
the Trade Descriptions Act if they kept calling it a
Cheap Day Return. We got Awayday. Now they daren't
even call us passengers, no, we're customers. We pay but
we don't necessarily travel . . . And do you remember
when things came in three sizes, small – it was just a
guess, sir – medium and large? Well, now, for the benefit
of my friend at the back, we have regular, large and
jumbo . . . I'd just got used to dropping the ham in
burger and now I'm supposed to ask for a Whopper –
sorry, again, at the back –'

'It's the quality, not the quantity,' a woman called
out.

I pulled a face. 'Oh, *get real*! . . .' I paused, and was
relieved to hear most of the rest of the women in the
audience laugh.

'It used to be easy ordering fish and chips and ketchup. I just don't know how to say filet-o-fish. I mean, is that a silent T and a long O, or what? . . . And that's before you get to the fries and BBQ dip – You what? Yeah, well, I can't see you, but I'd hazard a guess that you're a bit of a non-dairy creamer yourself . . . Oh, dear, there seems to be a wishy-washy liberal element in the audience tonight . . . as well as my friend the moronic git . . . or should I say PC? Remember when PC was your local policeman's first name? Remember local policemen? Well, now PC means politically correct. I'll try to explain . . . Do you remember the trouble you had persuading your mum not to call the bus conductor coloured? Remember bus conductors? Mine's just got used to saying black – slight hesitation first, she's not sure whether I'm pulling her leg – and now I'm telling her, "*No*, Mum, you've got to say Afro-Caribbean." I was quite happy being short, but they decided I was vertically challenged – What does that make you, sir? Genitally challenged, I expect . . .'

'Cunt!' he responded.

'I know your name, now what's the question?'

For the first time in months I wasn't getting the kind of adrenalin kick I usually get out of my stand-up routine. The heckler was relentless and drunk, but he was carrying some of the audience with him and had to be acknowledged. Normally they shut up if you keep lobbing back at them, but this one wouldn't. I was coping with him, just, but foul-mouthed back-chat wasn't really my thing. I vowed not to go on again without better preparation. Ad libbing was fine between characters, but I never wanted to do half an hour of it again.

It wouldn't have been so nerve-racking if I had arrived on time, but just as I was leaving my flat the phone had rung. I'd hesitated before answering it, because I was already a bit late and I normally like to have a drink at the pub and survey the opposition before starting. It was Agatha. She sounded absolutely terrible. I made her repeat her name three times before I recognized it. Her voice was so laboured that she had sounded like a heavy-breather.

'I know it's ... terrible thing to ask ... Saturday night ... bring yourself to come round ... think ... something wrong ... doesn't matter ...'

She was drunk. I had heard her speak like this to her clients on many an afternoon after a long lunch in Orso's and I recognized the rhythm, although I couldn't really understand what she was saying. After a week in which I had acted professionally beyond the call of duty, I thought it was a bit too much to be telephoned at home, so I told her that I was on my way out and suggested that she make herself a cup of tea and go to bed. I felt I was being quite polite in the circumstances. I said good-bye and see you on Monday. There was a long pause before she heaved a sigh and hung up. At least, I think that that is what happened. I've given it a lot of thought since and asked myself why I was so intolerant. The fact is, if I had known what she was going through I would have gone round straight away, but I didn't

Greg was standing by the bar. He handed me a gin and tonic.

'Did you see me?' I asked, rather hoping that he hadn't.

'Only the last bit ... Your man at the back was giving you a lot of trouble, wasn't he? You were fine though,' he added, and kissed me.

I liked the way he didn't exaggerate. A lot of actors

would have been all over me with compliments, their fingers firmly crossed behind their backs.

Later, in Khan's, I said, 'You're not like a lot of actors.'

'What do you mean?'

I took a mouthful of Chicken Tikka Masala on nan and thought about my response. As I was chewing, a small Hispanic-looking man approached our table bearing an armful of red roses individually wrapped in cellophane. He held one out to Greg, indicating that he should buy it for me.

'Would you like it?' Greg asked.

'No thanks! Absolutely not! God, they're so intrusive. I have no idea how they make a living, do you?' I rattled on, to cover my embarrassment. 'I mean, have you ever seen anyone actually buy one of those roses?'

The rose vendor had moved on to the table beside us, where a couple were munching pappadoms. Without hesitation, the man took a pound coin from his pocket and exchanged it for a rose for his girlfriend.

Greg and I both laughed.

'That's obviously how they make a living,' said Greg.

I slurped my lager and tried to remember what I had been saying before we were interrupted.

'Well, as I was saying, the actors I know are usually pretty vain, self-important –'

'Yeah, the list is endless! I don't really think of myself as an actor. I'm good-looking, so I might as well use it. When I lose that, I'm going to concentrate more on writing.'

'But you won't lose it!' I was shocked by the matter-of-fact way he had described himself. It was so un-English. No false modesty and yet not a trace of arrogance.

'Oh, I will. You should see my father. I'm the dead

ringer for him in his twenties, but time and the booze . . .
Even if I'm careful I'll puff out. Now, be honest, would
you still be sitting here with me if I –'

'Yes!' It sounded so positive and uncool, we both
laughed, although when I thought about it afterwards I
wondered if I had been entirely truthful. I didn't really
know him. There was an instinctive sympathy between
us, but we hadn't had a chance to test each other's
minds. I was in love with his looks, his voice and his
smile. He appeared to be a good person. That was all I
had to go on.

I've always thought that necking in a taxi is a bit
immature. With Greg it seemed like an urgent need. If
the journey had been slightly longer, and I hadn't been
wearing leggings, who knows what would have happened? Answer: I do, because we fucked on the stairs on
the way up to my flat, as well as more leisurely inside.

We ended up lying on the living-room floor with the
duvet wrapped around us.

Suddenly he said, 'This is a bit intense, isn't it?'

I started to feel the beginnings of a sense of unease.

'What do you mean? I mean, I know the meaning of
intense, but it looks like you are trying to say something
else.' I was already getting ready for the standard speech
about not wanting to get too committed, pressure etc.,
etc.

'I just meant it's surprisingly intense,' he said, quite
calmly. 'Considering we don't really know each other. I
kind of feel we do, though. Do you know what I'm
talking about?'

Relieved, I said that I did, and we both laughed and
hugged. It felt very safe and cosy.

'It's just that,' he went on, 'it's just that I feel I ought
to tell you that I'm kind of seeing someone else.'

I looked at him disbelievingly. After all that we had just done, this seemed a particularly cruel and inappropriate moment. I swallowed tears and said in the iciest voice I could muster, 'Oh, I see. Well, I guess you'd better go, then.'

He looked surprised and wounded by my tone.

'If you would just let me —'

'Oh, for God's sake, don't give me the speech about giving you some time. I've heard that speech. Listen, Greg, just go. You've picked the wrong person to do this to. I don't need this and I'm not going to have it. So next time you fancy a fuck, don't talk about how intense it feels.'

'Explain. I was going to say that if you would let me explain.'

'I don't want to hear. I'm sorry, it might do your guilty conscience some good, but it won't help me at all. It was fun and we didn't get involved. So let's just end it now, all right?'

'No. Not all right. I want you to hear what I have to say.'

'But I don't want to listen. Please go.' My voice was rising.

'OK. OK. I'm just sorry that you have to be so black and white about this. It seems such a waste.'

'Maybe it does, to you. But I have to protect myself, you know.'

'You've obviously been hurt.'

'Ten out of ten. That's why you shouldn't do this with people you don't know well. You know, I made a rule for myself a while back never to sleep with a man on the first date. It never works because you know each other physically too quickly, and you never catch up emotionally —'

83

'Well, we did it before we even had a date,' he interrupted.

I had to laugh. 'I wonder if that counts as breaking the rule, then?'

The atmosphere had become a little bit more relaxed. He was kissing me again, but this time with a kind of protective affection. For a moment I forgot about the someone else.

'I'm sorry, Greg, but we can't do this,' I said, remembering.

'Another rule?'

'Yup, I'm afraid so.'

He got up and started putting on his clothes. I stayed under the duvet, reluctant to be naked in front of him again, and feeling very vulnerable. He bent down and kissed me on my forehead.

'Ring me if you change your mind,' he said, and then let himself out.

One of my hands came out from hiding under the quilt and waved. I was too choked to say anything. When the door closed, I started to cry.

I woke up on Sunday feeling miserable. My mouth tasted of stale curry and however much I brushed my teeth I couldn't get rid of the flavour, constantly reminding me of the evening before. I had nothing to do, so I whiled away the day in bed, sometimes flicking through the channels on telly, sometimes dozing. In the late afternoon, I put on my track suit and ran round the Inner Circle in Regent's Park a couple of times. What I have never understood about exercise is, if it does you so much good, why do you concoct so many excuses not to do it? As usual, having run for about half an hour my mood lifted. It was getting dark as I walked back down

Regent's Park Road, a cold, clear November evening. As I neared Primrose Hill I realized, because of the teeming multitudes of people, that tonight was the night of the Primrose Hill Residents' Association bonfire. All of London seemed to be there. At the gates of Primrose Hill Park, the good and great of Camden were standing holding out buckets to collect money for the fireworks. There were a couple of tradesmen selling narrow plastic tubes filled with fluorescent liquid to the children of the more gullible parents of NW3 to wear as necklaces, but they weren't doing much business. I was half tempted to stay and watch, but I had a party in Hampstead to go to, with fewer fireworks, but more people I knew, and tonight I needed company.

I lay in hot water and sandalwood oil feeling happier and more relaxed. After a few minutes the phone started ringing. I sighed and made a resolution to get a cordless one as soon as I could afford it, so that I could bathe at the same time as talk. I sank deeper into the water so that my ears were submerged and my hair drifted away from my face. But the ringing continued. I wished I had turned on my answerphone and reluctantly got out of the bath. By this time I had convinced myself it must be Greg and I was trying to shake myself into a suitably intransigent mood to deal with him. Needless to say, the second I bent to pick the receiver up the ringing stopped. I picked it up anyway, only to hear the dialling tone. It reminded me of Agatha's call the day before. I felt a little anxious about how off-hand I had been and, since her flat was almost *en route*, I decided to call round to see her on my way to the party.

I put on my favourite little black dress, black opaque tights, ankle boots and lots of large fake pearls. I was just leaving the house wearing my trenchcoat, when I decided that it wasn't going to rain that night and I swapped it for a ludicrous swing coat I had bought two years before on a business trip to New York. It's made of pink fake fur and has Mickey Mouse faces imprinted in black all over it. I had to walk as far as Belsize Park to get a taxi because the roads were full of traffic.

There was no answer to the bell. I rang several times and was just about to leave, with a clear conscience, when I felt the touch of a furry animal around my legs. I jumped and narrowly avoided treading on the tail of Chutney, Agatha's cat. It is an unmistakable cat. I have never encounter one so large. Agatha would often come into the office with Chutney draped around her neck like a live stole. Like most cats, he is extremely friendly when he wants something and totally aloof otherwise. He obviously wanted to get into the building. I was explaining out loud that there was no one home, when I remembered that I had a set of Agatha's keys in my bag.

. The lift creaked its way to the fourth floor. Chutney followed me down the passage and I let us both into the flat. Inside the corridor was dark but there was light coming from the kitchen at the end. I called out, 'Hallo?'

No answer.

'Hallo? Agatha?'

Still nothing.

I began to feel a little like a burglar. Agatha had obviously gone out and forgotten to turn off the lights. I should have just left then, but for some reason I decided to go down to the kitchen and turn off the light. The door to the day room was open and the cat disappeared into the darkness inside. The other doors were shut, as they had been before. Nothing seemed unusual until I got to the kitchen.

It was sparkling clean. All the debris of Wednesday had been cleared up. The lino floor was white and shiny. I hadn't been able to distinguish its colour before. The surfaces had been scrubbed and there was a powerful smell of bleach. The rubbish bin, which had been over-flowing, was empty and resting upside-down on the draining board. I smiled as I envisaged Agatha with an apron and mop. I turned off the light and was walking back towards the door when curiosity got the better of me. There was obviously no one at home and I couldn't resist a peek at the other rooms. I opened the first door on the right and switched on the light. It was a huge bathroom with an enormous cast-iron bath with claw feet standing in the centre. I opened the next door. The lamp by the bed was on and it threw a soft golden light around the room. I didn't really have time to take in the decorations because lying diagonally across the top of the large double bed was Agatha, staring at me.

'Look, I'm terribly sorry,' I started to say. 'I was a bit concerned about you, and I don't know why really, but I decided to come round, then I remembered that I had your keys and well, your cat seemed to want to come in, and it's cold out there, and . . .'

I realized mid-sentence that her expression hadn't changed at all.

'Are you all right? I mean, I know that it's an intrusion, and, yes, I suppose I was being a bit nosy, but . . .'

Still no change. I began to feel extremely nervous. I took a side-step. Her eyes did not move. I began to panic. I was feeling rather embarrassed at conversing with her when her kimono-like dressing gown was gaping open, so I picked up a towel from the floor and ap-proached the bed, holding it out like a toreador's cape in front of me. When I was as near as I dared I threw it

87

over her body. It covered her up to her breasts. Still she lay trance-like in the same position.

I must have seen hundreds of situations similar to the one I was in on television, or in films, but for several minutes I stood frozen by Agatha's bed, wanting to be anywhere else in the world, with absolutely no idea what to do. I couldn't bring myself to touch her and yet I didn't feel she was dead. She was rather yellow in colour but it wasn't a deathly pallor. After a while I knelt down by the side of the bed and watched her chest. I couldn't tell whether she was breathing or whether I was imagining it. There was a half-finished mug on the bedside table – it smelt of whisky and lemons – and next to it a telephone.

I dialled 999.

14

The Casualty area of the Royal Free is not the most pleasant place to spend a night. The ambulance arrived at about nine o'clock and Agatha was wheeled on a stretcher into one of the resuscitation wards. After a few minutes a female doctor came out to talk to me. I was struggling with a form they had given me and feeling miserably inadequate. Apart from her name, I was unable to fill in any of the details it requested about Agatha, not even her age. I tried to explain who I was, and why I had been in the flat. Whatever came out of my mouth must have sounded very odd, because the doctor decided to continue the conversation in one of the anterooms surrounded by curtains.

'Now, try to think,' she said very calmly. 'If you're not her next of kin, who is?'

'Is she dead?' The words 'next of kin' triggered that response in me.

'No. But she is not well at all. Please try to think who we should contact.'

I thought. I knew only one person who was close to Agatha and that was Anthony White. I said his name.

'And what relation is he to the patient?'

'Well, business partner, I suppose.'

'You don't know of any relations?'

'Well, she has a sister. But they don't —'

'And what's her name?' the doctor interrupted.

'Dorothy.'

'Is that Dorothy Brown?'

'I suppose so. No, wait a minute, she's married. I suppose she's from the generation that would have changed their names.'

The doctor began to look exasperated.

'I'm trying to think.' I knew it began with B. I had typed it on to the computer several times the week before, but my mind had gone blank.

The doctor left me for a minute and when she came back in I remembered.

'It's Burton. No, I've no idea where she lives. I imagine London. Can you tell me what's happening?'

'I'm afraid there's nothing much I can tell you at present. You just wait outside for a moment.'

It seemed like hours before she came back. The waiting room was filling up with the casualties of Guy Fawkes Night. Several sets of parents were holding children with burnt limbs. One little boy had been brought in with blood streaming from his eye, which was blackened with soot. He was rushed away and his screams echoed down the corridor.

Finally the doctor reappeared.

'We have managed to locate the next of kin. You can go home now. Would you like me to give you a sedative to help you sleep?'

'No, I'd like to stay, if I may.'

'I don't really think I would advise it.'

That made me even more determined.

'Can you prevent me from staying?'

'No, I can't. I just wouldn't advise it.' She looked me up and down with some distaste. It was only then that I realized I must look rather odd, sitting on a hard chair in that tatty, soulless room, wearing my party outfit, complete with bright-pink Mickey Mouse coat. But I didn't feel I could just go. I knew I was in the way, but I couldn't leave until I knew that Agatha was all right.

I must have fallen asleep at around midnight. Most of the wounded children had been dealt with by then and the waiting room had a new population of victims. They were young men who had drunk too much and ended up in pub brawls. A couple of tramps slunk in surreptitiously and lay down over several chairs, but they were ushered out by extremely patient auxiliary nurses who looked as if they were well practised. I had read all the depressing notices on the walls several times. I knew the number of the AIDS hotline practically off by heart. The coffee machine didn't work. I had tried to call my mother, but remembered only after about twenty unanswered rings that she and Reg would be in Madeira by now. In the end I gave in to the shock and boredom and nodded off.

I awoke with a start. The clock said nine-fifteen, but it had been saying that all evening. I looked at my watch. It was one-thirty. The waiting room was empty and there was no one at the reception desk. I heard the familiar diesel rumble of a taxi drawing away outside and then Agatha walked in through the entrance. She didn't seem to see me, but marched straight to reception. I got up, feeling a little dizzy from my doze, and approached her. I said hallo. She turned round and I realized that I was mistaken. The woman standing in front of me was considerably shorter than Agatha. Her face was almost exactly the same shape, but smoother and softer and there was no look of recognition on it.

'Dorothy?' I ventured.

'Have we met?' She replied in the tone one would use at a county sherry party.

'No, we haven't.' I held out my hand. 'I'm Sophie Fitt. I work with Ag . . . Miss Brown.'

'Oh, you were the one who brought her in?'

'Yes.'

'I'm sorry that I have taken so long to get here, but I live on the other side of London.' She was speaking very slowly and carefully. I wondered if she always spoke like that, or if it had to do with the alcohol I could smell around her, which she had tried to mask, not very effectively, with perfume and mouthwash.

A nurse appeared and I went over to her and explained who Dorothy was. She scuttled off and returned with a male doctor. I wondered whether they had changed shifts. He ignored me and took Dorothy off into the curtained side-room. He had a very loud voice, though, and the curtains couldn't prevent me hearing bits of the conversation.

'Afraid . . . bad news . . . we did try everything . . . too far gone . . . very sorry.'

'Oh, I see.' Three simple, emotionless words from Dorothy.

I found that I was shaking. I went to sit down. The curtains were drawn back and through watery eyes I saw Dorothy and the doctor walking away down the corridor. They looked an incongruous couple. He was wearing a white coat and walking slowly, as if bowed down by worry; her coat was almost ankle-length and black, and the tap of her shiny black heels reverberated eerily in the silence. Suddenly she turned round, remembering that I was there, and came back to me.

'It seems that my sister died about ten minutes ago. Thank you for waiting. I'm afraid there is nothing more to be done.'

'How?'

'They think it looks like an overdose. I'm going back to the flat now with the police. They have to look around.'

And with that she turned and walked away.

I can't remember much about getting home. I suppose I must have walked. I can recall hearing the occasional whoosh of rockets in the air and seeing the sky go momentarily red as they exploded. But I don't know whether I am transposing those images from earlier on that night. I have no sense of what time it was when I rang Martin. In fact, when he rang me the next day, I couldn't even remember leaving a message on his machine. For several hours I must have been in almost total blackout and when I was awakened by my phone ringing at eight in the morning I was sure that I had been having a terrible nightmare.

'Miss Fitt?'

'Yes.'

'I'm sorry if I woke you.'

'That's OK. Who is this?'

'Mr Middlemarch. I'm the Coroner's Officer. The Royal Free have been in touch with me and given me your name.'

'Yes?'

'I believe that you brought Miss Brown to the hospital and I'm afraid I have to ask you some questions for my report.'

'Oh.' It wasn't a nightmare then. The night before was gradually forcing itself back into my consciousness. I had no idea what he expected me to say. There was a heavy silence.

'Could you give me a convenient time for the interview?'

My mind was whirling. Was it still the weekend? No, it was Monday. I was due at work in an hour. Or was I? My boss was dead, I suddenly realized. I didn't know whether that meant I even had a job.

'I'm sorry,' I said, 'I'm a bit confused. Do you mean you want to interview me?'

'Yes.' He sounded very patient. 'At your convenience. Would ten o'clock suit you?'

'Today?'

'This morning, yes.'

'Where?'

'I could come to your home.'

'Look,' I said, 'I'm terribly sorry, but I don't really understand what's going on.'

'Can I make a suggestion?' said Mr Middlemarch.

'By all means.' It seemed a ridiculous conversation to be having with a complete stranger.

'I'll ring you back in a few minutes, when you've had time to have a cup of coffee.'

'Oh, thanks. Fine. Bye, then.'

I put down the phone. I got up and went to the bathroom. I caught a glimpse of myself in the mirror and saw that I was still fully dressed for the party. For some strange reason I felt guilty for not having rung my hosts to say that I wasn't coming. I was about to pick up the phone when I realized that Paul and Jennifer would already have set off for their jobs in the City. I went back to the bathroom and splashed water on my face. It made last night's make-up look worse, but I felt a bit better. The phone rang again. I toyed with the idea of not answering it. I didn't really want to deal with Mr Middlemarch again, but he had sounded rather firm, albeit polite, and I felt obliged to pick it up.

'Quick cup of coffee!' I said as cheerily as I could.

'Soph, are you OK?' It was Martin.

'Oh, sorry, Martin, I thought you were the Coroner's Officer.'

'Soph. What the hell is going on?'

His voice sounded so concerned and reassuring that I immediately burst into tears. I couldn't get out any words at all, because once the crying started, it came out in great moaning blubs and I couldn't stop it.

'Soph. Listen to me. I'm coming round, right now. Just hang on till I get there, please. Soph, do you hear. I'll be there as soon as I can. Do you hear?'

I managed something that sounded like yes.

By the time Mr Middlemarch called again, I had composed myself a bit, made a cup of coffee, as he had instructed, and had just finished drinking it.

I told him that he could come round at ten. I rang work and spoke to Janet. She said that the police had been and that Anthony was ringing the major clients. She was going to field calls, but she had no idea what to tell people. She sounded almost excited, as if it were a major intrigue in her favourite soap opera, which, in a way, I suppose it was. I told her to tell Anthony that I was taking the day off, if he asked.

Mr Middlemarch had the demeanour of someone familiar with death. He was a tall man of uncertain age with grey hair, not unlike John Major with a moustache. I have never met an undertaker, but when I do I imagine he will resemble Mr Middlemarch. Behind the obsequious concern in his voice, however, there was a steel-like impassive quality that made me feel quite nervous.

I offered him coffee but he declined. As I cleared a space on my dining table, which was covered in unread Sunday newspapers, I noticed him surveying the room quite carefully as if taking mental notes. Then he started questioning me in his monotonous voice. We got through my details quite quickly and then he asked me to describe the events of the preceding evening. To my horror, I giggled. Partly through nerves and partly because it seemed such a clichéd phrase.

'You sound just like a policeman in a film,' I said pathetically, in explanation.

'I am an officer of the law,' he replied levelly. 'It's my job to investigate any death that occurs in unnatural circumstances.'

Suddenly our meeting took on a whole different meaning. I realized that I was about to give a police statement and it terrified me. Especially since I needed to start off with an explanation of why I was at the flat, which I felt amounted to breaking and entering. I wished that Martin would arrive. By this time I had so little faith in my judgement, I was beginning to doubt that he had called at all.

'Do you mind if I just go to the toilet?' I said, playing for time.

'Not at all.'

I sat on the toilet for as long as was decently possible, but came to no conclusion.

'What do they think happened to Agatha?' I said, coming back into the room.

'That's what we are trying to establish,' he replied noncommittally.

I saw I had no choice but to begin and I described very plainly what I could remember. When I got to the end he thanked me and said there were just a few questions he wanted to ask.

'Did Miss Brown, to your knowledge, drink to excess.'

I said that she drank quite a lot, but that I wasn't sure how much excess would constitute. I felt I was becoming as pedantic as he was.

'Was she, to your knowledge, very unhappy?'

96

'Do you mean they think she killed herself?'

'Do you find that shocking?'

I thought about it.

'Yes, I do, actually. I just wouldn't have imagined she was the type, but then I didn't know her very well . . . Was there a note?'

'I'm sorry, but I am not at liberty to disclose that information.'

I was beginning to find the interview frustrating. He was asking my opinion, but refusing to give me the information on which to base it. If she had left a note, then wouldn't it have been obvious that she was unhappy? Perhaps that was why he had asked, because there wasn't a note. Whether there was or not, I felt it was disrespectful to be discussing Agatha's supposed motives only hours after she had died with someone who had never met her.

'We did find this.' He held out a small piece of yellow paper. 'On a pad next to her bed. Does it mean anything to you?'

I took the piece of paper from his hand and recognized it as a Post-it note. On it was scrawled in capital letters 'SOPHIE LIST'.

It was Agatha's scratchy writing.

I looked at it for a long time as if some meaning would leap out of the paper.

'Perhaps she was making a list of things for me to do on Monday. I really don't know. As I said, she did ring me on Saturday, just as I was going out, but I couldn't understand what she wanted.'

'She was drunk?'

'Yes. That's what it sounded like. What did she die of?'

'The post-mortem will tell. For the moment I don't

think I would be disclosing anything improper if I said that there seems to have been a lot of alcohol and painkillers in her blood.'

'Poor Agatha,' I said.

We sat in silence as he wrote out my statement. I read it through and signed it. Then he thanked me and left. He hadn't got to the bottom of the stairs when my entryphone rang again.

'Who on earth was that zombie?' said Martin a minute later.

I laughed with relief at seeing a familiar face.

'That was Mr Middlemarch, the Coroner's Officer.'

'What the hell is going on, Soph? You look a complete wreck. You leave a message in the middle of the night, at least I think it's you, because you didn't even leave your name, then you're in tears when I call, and then you're entertaining an undead to breakfast. Heavy night, was it?'

'That's one way of putting it,' I said, and started to explain again.

15

Relating events for a second time seemed to give them a kind of reality they hadn't had before. Martin didn't get the edited version, but was subjected to a minute-by-minute account. It was lunchtime before I had finished and I could see that he was getting a little agitated.

'I've only told them at the bank that I'm taking the morning off,' he explained. 'We've got quite a big pitch going on. I'd better be getting back.'

'But you can't.' I felt on the verge of tears again, as I had sporadically throughout my account.

'OK, OK. Let me use your phone and I'll call them.'

I felt uncomfortable listening to him telling his boss that he would be delayed. I knew how tough Jerry could be, and Martin was not explaining the situation very well, as he was trying to avoid using my name.

'I'm going to take you out for a nice lunch,' said Martin, as he put down the phone.

'I don't feel very hungry.'

'Well, I do. And you should eat. It'll do you good to get out, anyway.'

I found that I was rather hungry after all when I smelt the charcoal and spice smells of the Cajun restaurant in Hampstead. I remembered that I hadn't really eaten anything since Saturday as I ordered a blackened chicken salad and deep-fried sweet potatoes. We sat at a window table, sipping tomato juice with a lot of Tabasco, in silence.

'What I don't understand,' I said finally, 'is why someone, especially Agatha, who is, was, not exactly houseproud, would clean up her kitchen before she killed herself.'

'What do you mean?'

'Well, you know I told you how I came to be in the flat? Well, the kitchen light was on and, when I went to turn it off, the kitchen was unrecognizable from how it was the other day.'

'Well, maybe you just saw it on a bad day.'

'Maybe.'

'Anyway, she may not have cleared it up herself. She probably has a cleaner.'

'True . . . But there's also the question of Chutney.'

'What?'

'Agatha's cat. He's called Chutney. Apparently he used to have a ginger brother called Marmalade. Anyway, why would Agatha want to be without Chutney?'

'I should think she probably had other things on her mind,' said Martin. 'Look, Soph, I know you feel bad about this – it is horrible to think that someone you know would want to kill herself – but it looks pretty clear that that is what she did, and the sooner you acknowledge it, the sooner you'll get over it.'

I pushed away the rest of my food.

'The thing is, the more I think about it, the more unlikely it seems. She just wasn't like that.'

'You don't know that, though. You said yourself that you didn't really know anything about her.'

'I'm allowed to have intuitions, though. You're talking as if I'm not involved. I am. I mean, I was the one who took her to hospital, and she wrote that note to me.'

'Honestly, Soph, I think that you're still a bit shocked. Two words is hardly a note, and she may have written it ages before, for all you know. I know it's not a very nice thing to have happened, but I think we should try to get you to think about something else.'

I gave in. He was probably right. We chatted falsely and awkwardly about trivia over coffee and then got up to leave. It was already getting dark and there was a cruel November wind. Martin suggested that we take a cab back to my place and that I go to bed and try to get some sleep. He was offering to stay when I interrupted him.

'I think I'll just go and have a look round Agatha's flat.'

'Soph, you can't. You're being silly now. What could you possibly find there? The police have probably swept it. Anyway, I'm sure it would be illegal.'

'I've still got the keys.'

'Soph, you can't.'

'I can. It's a matter of whether or not I'm prepared to. Well, I just want to put my mind at rest, that's all. I want to see if there is a list of things she wants, wanted me to do. You needn't come. I'll be all right.'

Martin looked exasperated. He knows me well enough to know that I can be very stubborn.

'Please don't. As a favour to me?' he pleaded.

Nothing looked any different from the night before except that the mug by the bed had been taken away, leaving a ring on the wooden surface. On the table at the other side of the bed were Agatha's fountain pen, without its distinctive Mont Blanc cap, and a blank Post-it note pad from which I imagine the police had torn the note Mr

Middlemarch had shown me. The day room looked just as it had during the week, with piles of files and papers everywhere, but I couldn't see any form of list for me. The door of the sideboard was open and, as I went to close it, I saw that of the nine full bottles of Glenmorangie there had been on Wednesday, only six remained. The cat was asleep on the gold velvet *chaise-longue*. I was just wondering who was going to look after him when we heard the sound of keys in the door. Martin, in an action that seems hilarious in retrospect, dashed into the bathroom for cover. I was standing frozen in the day room when Dorothy walked in.

'Hallo,' I said, as naturally as possible. 'I just came round to see if there's any work to pick up.'

'Oh. I'm only here to pick up the cat. Somebody's got to look after him. Although Jack will kill me, because he's allergic to them.'

'Right then,' I said. It occurred to me only later that Dorothy, who was next of kin and had every right to be in the flat, was behaving as nervously as I, who had no right whatsoever.

'I came with a friend,' I said. 'He's just using the toilet. I hope that's OK?'

'Of course.'

'Oh. Well, then. I'll just take this lot,' I said, pointing randomly at a pile of papers, on top of which lay Agatha's dictation machine. 'Anthony asked me to pick anything up, you know, just to tidy up loose ends,' I elaborated.

'I didn't think you would be in the office today,' Dorothy observed coolly.

'I wasn't,' I stuttered. 'But he phoned.'

'I see. Yes, well. He always was thorough,' she added with disdain.

I breathed a sigh of relief. I had almost been caught in a lie. It was time to go. I knocked on the bathroom door.

'Martin? I'm ready. Are you going to be all day?' I shouted, rather more loudly than was necessary. The door opened so quickly that it was obvious Martin had been listening through the keyhole. Luckily Dorothy was still in the day room.

We managed to contain ourselves as far as the lift, but as soon as it started going down we both burst out laughing. The last five minutes had been so tense.

'I don't know why you gave up acting, Soph. You could have won an Oscar for that performance.'

'Yes, and where were you when I needed you?'

Martin returned my glare.

'Don't even think about pursuing the damsel in distress line with me,' he said. 'It was entirely your fault that we were in there anyway.'

'OK.' I held up my hands in defeat.

'Did it set your mind to rest, then?' he asked, as we walked past the rubbish bins and down the drive to the road.

'I suppose so. I still can't get used to it though.'

'Well, it is only twenty-four hours since it happened. Come on, let's have a drink at the Flask.'

16

I woke up very early on Tuesday morning thinking I had had a terrible nightmare again. This time, when it sank in, I felt empty and depressed. I made myself some coffee and toast like an automaton and sat at my table trying to distract myself by reading the Sunday papers. After several minutes I found that I had read nothing. The words swam around on the page. I didn't seem to be able to order them. I lay in the bath until I realized that I was shivering with cold and I tried on several outfits before deciding what to wear. Having run over the events of Sunday night in my mind almost to the point of exhaustion, my brain now turned itself to Saturday and the phone conversation I had had with Agatha. The more I remembered, the more pain I felt. If I hadn't been so bloody selfish I might possibly have saved her life. But why on earth had she called me? Surely she had friends she could talk to. Or was she so obsessed with her work that she wanted to give me a list of tasks to clear up before she died? But then, why kill herself? Whatever, I had failed her.

The guilt was becoming unbearable and I felt angry with myself and everyone else. I cursed my mother and Reg for being away. I wanted to be given the sort of embrace only a family can give, to be told that it wasn't my fault. But the more I thought about it, the more I felt it was.

Eventually I forced myself to go in to the office. I

couldn't endure tormenting myself any longer. At least outside I could turn the anger I felt towards myself against somebody else, as the taxi driver discovered after he had made the mistake of saying, 'Cheer up, love, it may never happen!'

To my surprise, the office turned out to be a haven that day. It was easier to be with people who knew Agatha. Janet was extremely solicitous, although I thought, rather uncharitably, that her motives had as much to do with gleaning all the details as with my welfare. She told me that I looked terrible and made me several cups of tea before getting back to her work. She was sitting at my desk using the word-processing facility on the computer for the first time, because she was having to type the same letter to all the clients. After a while she said, 'It's fantastic this machine.'

I nodded, silently accepting the proffered olive branch.

'Is Anthony in?' I asked.

'Yes, but he has his door closed,' she said solemnly.

'Well, I can see that!'

'There's no need to be clever about it. I think he's having difficulty keeping it all together. He had his door closed yesterday too. He said he was calling the clients, but he looked very red in the eye to me. They were very close, you know,' she added in a hushed whisper, and held up her hand with two fingers crossed.

'You don't mean . . .'

'Well, I've never been told officially, but I wouldn't be surprised.'

'But, but . . . Agatha was so much more sophisticated.' The words were out before I had a chance to censor them. At least I didn't add that I had always assumed Janet herself was having an affair with Anthony.

'You mean older? I don't think there's more than five years in it. Anthony, of course, looks a lot younger.'

I didn't really agree. I thought of Agatha as rather timeless and Anthony as a man in his early fifties trying to look younger. But it was pointless to discuss it further. Janet seemed to feel that there were two sides to the relationship, whatever it was, between Agatha and Anthony, and that she was on his. I decided to take the post into Agatha's office, since Janet was at my desk and I didn't want anything to distract her from her new-found love of the computer.

I couldn't stop thinking about Anthony and Agatha having an affair. I found myself rather repelled by the idea. Surely she could have chosen someone better? Or perhaps not. I was starting to think of her as someone who had lived rather an empty life, for all its surface glamour. It was beginning to be less of a shock that she had decided to end it.

I gazed around her office. It occurred to me that all the messages of thanks and photographs on her wall, which I had previously found so attractive, might be nothing more than material props to boost an empty soul. In the end, what had Agatha achieved, other than helping along other people's success? It was a vicarious existence. Ostensibly sociable but ultimately lonely. Here was her enormous Victorian drawered desk separating her from her clients, symbol of power and distance. In the cold half-light of a winter's day there was nothing hospitable about the office. The blob lamp was off, its glass bulb filled with static mauvy-grey fluid.

I sat in the chair where Chutney used to spend his days sleeping and thought about how little you ever know someone else. I had described Agatha on countless occasions to my friends, using words like individual, confident, brilliant and, when she had pissed me off, arrogant, selfish, opinionated. Now I had so many conflicting ideas about her I couldn't fix a picture in my mind, except the image of her in a coma which kept leaping to the front of my mind when I least expected it and making me gulp with horror.

I thought about the odd bond we seemed to have forged between us and the strange coincidence that she had known my father better than I ever had. Considering that we had been acquainted for a bare two months, I had felt surprisingly close to her, as if she were part of my life and had always been. But this was all my assumption, because I hadn't known her really at all, hadn't understood the pain she was suffering, hadn't ever imagined that she was anything other than the brightly coloured, eccentric, engaging exterior she showed the world. Finally, tears which somehow hadn't come before started rolling down my cheeks, for Agatha and for the helplessness of human beings.

I wiped my face. I had been staring, without realizing that I was, at the array of published plays on Agatha's shelves. I hadn't noticed before, and was surprised, since Agatha was rather disorganized, that they were placed in alphabetical order. I worked my way back from Y (none of her clients' names began with Z) up the alphabet. There must have been several hundred books. I opened the library chair which converted into a set of steps and climbed up to view the top row.

I suddenly thought how very ungenerous I was being. Agatha was the sort of agent who really did change things. Writers and actors needed the sort of support she was so good at giving. Looking at her client list was like reading a potted history of British and Irish theatre over the last thirty years. If she had chosen to throw herself into that, then I ought to be admiring her, not criticizing. The library of plays was an awe-inspiring epitaph. If I were to die suddenly, I thought, there would be nothing at all to show for my life. Not even a grieving partner. So who was I to judge? I began to cry harder and harder until I was almost hyperventilating. Then suddenly I gasped, and stopped, as you do. I felt I wanted to cry more, but I couldn't. I was face to face with the blue and white ceramic horse that stood on the top shelf. I had admired it before on many occasions as I looked around the room when Agatha was on the phone, but I had never seen it close to. It was a beautiful object, probably Turkish in origin; its height matched almost perfectly the depth of the top shelf. What I hadn't seen from my usual position below the shelves was that the horse was standing on a slim paperback book. Slowly, I picked the horse up and slid the book out. The outer rim of it was covered in dust, but the characteristic Penguin blocking and the sanserif black typeface showed through. The title was *The Hairs in the Sink*.

I brushed off the dust, replaced the horse and climbed down the steps.

The spine cracked as I opened the book and the pages smelt musty. I began to read.

The copyright line was 1962, the year of my birth, and underneath it a sentence announced that one should apply to Brown and Brown for performance rights.

There were four characters in the play: two women, Jemima and Bella, who share a large house in south London, their servant and general factotum Sid, and Johnny, a young man from Merseyside who arrives, in the first scene, to rent a room.

Although the form seemed to be very much like several other of the angry-young-man plays I was familiar with – young working-class man, too intelligent and ambitious for his home town, leaves to better himself and finds himself encountering two women, one attractive, usually older, sophisticated and worldly, the other beautiful, innocent, undoubtedly middle class and ultimately his ruin – the setting was much more Gothic and fantastical, a kind of Norma Desmond meets Jimmy Porter in Dulwich Village.

I found myself enjoying the first scene. The dialogue crackled. The two women, both obviously attracted to the rough but very good-looking young man, question him mercilessly about his background and mock his accent. At one point Jemima remarks in an aside to Bella, 'He's rather unfinished, don't you think? Shall we finish him?'

They decide to give him the room, although it is unclear why he would want it after this grilling, much to the pique of Sid, who has been popping in and out delivering tea, and the odd waspish remark, throughout.

Scene two was set in a bedroom, where the two women are going through a huge wardrobe of clothes, trying each outfit on as if they are children dressing up. Jemima has a particular liking for shoes. The language she uses to describe each pair is lyrical, like love poetry. The stage direction at the side of the text reads: 'It is obvious that none of the shoes fits her feet.' Was this a reference to Cinderella, I wondered, and turned another page.

I don't know how long Anthony had been watching me. I became aware of his presence just before he spoke. I sat up abruptly (I had made myself comfortable on the leopardskin sofa) and shoved the book under a cushion. I felt as if I had been caught reading in bed after lights-out.

'Thank you for coming in to work,' he said. I couldn't detect any trace of sarcasm in his voice.

I turned towards the door. I'm not sure why, but Englishmen look good in mourning, and Anthony was no exception. The suit was well cut and his shirt was crisp and freshly laundered. Black made him appear slimmer too. It was such a difference that I almost complimented him, but realized just in time that it would be inappropriate.

'It must have been an awful shock for you,' he said. 'I've known her so long, nothing that she did would shock me ...' He smiled weakly and started walking towards me. I stood up, flustered, hoping that he wasn't about to hug me, as Janet had done when I arrived. But he walked past me and went and sat in Agatha's chair behind her desk. It made me feel very uncomfortable to see him there.

'Look, love,' he said slowly, 'I know we've had our differences, but I hope you'll stay on now that she's gone. We could do with some help. I am proposing to try to keep all the clients. We may already be too late for some of them. Bad news travels fast in this world. I expect that our competitors have already been on the phone to the stars.'

He had begun to speak quite animatedly, as if relishing the prospect of a tug-of-war with his rivals. For me, there was an unseemly haste about his actions. Like a widower announcing his marriage plans before his wife had been buried. And I hated the word 'stars'. It made him sound like a compère at a holiday camp.

He seemed to sense my distaste and continued solemnly, 'She was a formidable agent . . . and a formidable person. We will all miss her terribly.'

His voice cracked on the last sentence, and I realized that he was finding the conversation difficult. Beneath all the business-as-usual talk, he was deeply upset but, like most men, didn't want to show his emotions.

I didn't for a moment think that Anthony had any chance of holding on to the prestigious clients, who would always view him as second best, or to the group of young actors and directors Agatha had spent so much of her time encouraging and nurturing. There were any number of second-rate agents of his calibre in London, and very few individuals like Agatha. He certainly had a knack of packaging deals and claiming commission from as many sources as possible, but his client list was more game show than RSC, and I couldn't see any of my peers wanting to entrust their work to him. Perhaps that was why he was asking me to stay. It crossed my mind that if I played it right, there would be an opportunity for me to become an agent, but I couldn't bear the thought of Brown and Brown without Agatha, and I hadn't enough experience. I hadn't had a chance to think about what would happen to me. I had assumed that I would be there until the end of my contract in December. I didn't really want to stay, but I didn't really feel strong enough to look for another job either.

'All right, I'll stay,' I said, and smiled weakly.

'Thank you.' He paused. 'She was very fond of you, you know, said you brightened the place up. That was quite something for her. She despised her staff normally . . . She thought she would make a scriptwriter out of you.'

'Did she? But she didn't know anything about me.'

'Well, you know how she was,' he said.

'Yes,' I replied, although I was beginning to feel far from sure.

17

There was an obituary by Stuart Regan, one of the clients who had been with her since the 1960s, in the *Evening Standard*. It described their first meeting in a pub after a reading of his play *The Bomb*. She had been younger than him, and had barely started as an agent, but she had acted as if she owned the West End, and Broadway too. He wrote about her depth of knowledge and her taste, but most of all her ability to inspire others with confidence, which, he said, was her unique gift. She was one of the few agents whose commitment to the theatre remained with them through their success and the theatre would be diminished by her absence. I felt it was rather a dull piece by so eminent a writer, but supposed that it was a difficult duty to write an obituary. The last couple of lines stated that a memorial service was being arranged and would be announced at a later date.

The bus was nearing my stop, so I folded the paper, rang the bell and struggled to the front. I generally try to avoid public transport in London. For me the Underground is far too far underground ever to feel safe and the buses seem to be becoming smaller by the day. There's nothing worse than the press of unknown bodies just after you've woken up, or at the end of a long day, especially when you're about the height of most men's armpits. I chose to live in Primrose Hill partly because it is possible to walk in to most parts of Central London, although to be truthful I should think I have actually walked in less than five times, because there always seems to be a black cab passing with its orange light on, whether I need it or not. Today, however, I had deliberately waited for the Camden Hoppa (another reason I usually avoid the bus: I could as soon bring myself to say 'Must run for the Hoppa' as I could to order half a dozen Chicken McNuggets with BBQ dip) because I wanted to draw out my journey for as long as I could.

I was having dinner with Stephanie. She had invited me in the supermarket and I had forgotten to cancel, as I had intended, in the uproar of the last two days. I would have forgotten it completely had Stephanie not rung the office while I was talking with Anthony in Agatha's room to inquire whether I could tolerate dairy products.

In the end I was quite glad of the distraction. She had a new job doing PR for a company that specialized in holistic holidays. She had worked on various package-tour campaigns at the advertising agency where she had been since Cambridge. For me, there had been a rather odd disparity between her utterly commercial job and her back-to-nature life outside, and I thought that this would suit her better. She agreed that her Yin and Yang would be more balanced, and we settled down to our cauliflower cheese.

When I told her, over a cup of ginseng tea, what had been happening in my life since we last met, Stephanie turned out to be surprisingly helpful. One of her cousins had committed suicide and she had talked a lot about it in therapy. She knew all about the feelings of guilt and the strange numb sensation after a death. She insisted that I must be kind to myself and gave me some breathing exercises to do when I felt guilty. They must have worked, because I fell fast asleep on her sofa. I woke up feeling more relaxed than I had done for several days. She was chanting when I left, so I just touched her shoulder and let myself out.

Stephanie lives in Albert Street, off Parkway, and I found myself walking exactly the same route home as Greg and I had taken when we walked back from the wine bar. It had crossed my mind to ring him several times since the weekend, but I had not dared. Once we began talking I was pretty sure that one or other of us would suggest meeting and I couldn't allow myself to get involved. Particularly not when I was feeling so fragile. At the same time, I wished he would call me. It's rare to meet someone you're so completely physically in tune with, and I desperately wanted to spend a night wrapped round his body and to wake up looking at his face.

When I got back the phone was ringing. I could hear it from the bottom of the stairs. But as soon as I put the key in the lock it stopped. I suppose it might have been Greg. I consoled myself with the thought that it was probably Jerry, who had developed, since we broke up, an occasional habit of ringing me up drunk at about two in the morning and talking dirty down the phone. I didn't feel I could have coped with that.

The office was very quiet for the next couple of days. All of Agatha's clients seemed to have gone into mourning, except Paul Montefiore, who was no respecter of convention and rang, as he did almost every day, to ask where the hell his money was. I'm afraid the dumb-blonde-ever-so-obliging secretary act I normally affected for his benefit rather slipped, and I said what I had been longing to say to him for several weeks. Janet listened in amazement and gave me three cheers when I had finished.

'You ought to go into this business, you know,' she said.

'Hmm. The trouble is that you're meant to be like that with the opposition, not with your clients!'

'Well, he deserved it.'

'I hope Anthony won't mind losing him. Where is he, by the way?' I hadn't seen him since our chat on Tuesday evening and it was now Thursday morning.

'I think he's at the lawyers' again,' said Janet.

'Well, I wish he would hurry up. There's a huge pile of stuff on her desk that I can't deal with, and there's all this post. I need a bit of guidance. I mean, I don't even know how I should be responding to invitations now. Miss A. Brown regrets she won't be able to attend, or what?'

'It's not urgent, though, is it?'

'Well, not for her!'

Janet looked at me rather strictly, but then we both burst out laughing. Strangely, I seemed to have spent the last few days on the verge of tears or laughter. I suppose I was in a state somewhat akin to hysteria. It seemed terribly disrespectful to be laughing so near to Agatha's office, but somehow I didn't feel that she would have minded.

'By the way,' I said, wiping my eyes, 'when is the funeral?'

'Tomorrow. Family and close friends only. No flowers.'

'Oh. How do you know?' I felt I should have known too.

'Dorothy rang on Tuesday, just before you got in. She said that is what I should tell anyone who asked.'

'Is Anthony going?'

'I've no idea. I expect so. Although he and Dorothy, you know, never got on.'

'Could I go?'

'Would you want to?'

'Well, actually, I think I would.' I wasn't quite sure why, but I was rather hurt at not having been told.

'There's going to be a big memorial service, you know,' Janet said.

'Yes, I know, but I think I should have been asked.'

'Well, ring her up then.'

I took Dorothy's number and went into Agatha's room. The phone was answered by a man with a strong Liverpudlian accent. I assumed it was Jack Burton. I wondered whether to tell him that I was reading his play, but I didn't get the chance.

'Who wants her?' he shouted.

I said my name and hung on for a while, not knowing whether he was fetching Dorothy or had just left the phone hanging. Finally she spoke at the other end.

'What do you want?'

I was so taken aback I couldn't speak for a few seconds.

'I was wondering whether I could come to the funeral?' I finally said, no longer sure why I wanted to in the circumstances.

'It's really only for family, but I suppose ... Well, I can't really stop you, can I? Golders Green crematorium. Ten o'clock.'

And she put down the phone.

18

I doubt whether I would have gone to the funeral at all, if it hadn't been for a discussion I had at dinner that evening.

I have known Donny and Dan almost as long as they have known each other. They had already introduced themselves by the time I arrived at the Freshers' Footlights audition in our first term at Cambridge and they have been together ever since that day.

As Donny says, 'Thank God we didn't have to spend our first term in a crisis about our sexuality. We just saw each other and that was it. We knew we were a couple of old queens made for each other.'

At Cambridge I seemed to spend half my life in one or other of their rooms, drinking tea and eating good chocolate biscuits at Dan's, or champagne and canapés at Donny's. They were known as great hosts, and I counted them amongst my best friends. Since Cambridge we've drifted apart a little. They went on a grand tour of America in an old Cadillac for a couple of years, and when they came back to England they surprised everyone by buying a dilapidated farmhouse in Dorset and living there while Donny tried to do the place up and Dan wrote his first novel. Eventually Donny brought in a decorator and they managed to sell the house at a reasonable profit and move to London. Dan's first novel was published a while back in England, but apart from a few mixed reviews it achieved very little. The reason for the dinner party – 'That is, of course, if you ever need a reason for a dinner party', as Donny said as he opened the door – was that it had just been published in America, was the talk of the town and had reached the top twenty on the best-seller list. Paperback rights were being auctioned in New York even as we ate, and Dan's agent in New York was ringing every hour or so with an update on the price.

In the vast living room of their upper-ground-floor flat in Ladbroke Grove a huge banqueting table had been laid out for twenty or so guests. The room was candlelit by an enormous modern baroque chandelier hanging from a centre rose. A full-size palm tree in a terracotta pot stood in the curtainless bay window and two large gold-framed mirrors, the silvering bubbly and cracked, hung on facing sides of the room. The walls looked as if they had been stripped down to the plaster ready for painting, but I overheard Donny describing the effort it had taken to make them look like that – 'distressed' was the word he used – and realized that the effect was intentional. I knew about half the people in the room. I had arrived slightly late and was seated at the end of the table nearest to Dan, but furthest away from my friends.

'Here she is, at last!' said Donny, pulling out my chair. 'I hope she won't bore you too much.'

Dan smiled apologetically. He is by far the least flamboyant of the two and sometimes Donny's camp antics embarrass him.

Donny introduced me. The others around me were a literary editor; a rather shy female dentist, the new girlfriend of Donny's brother David, who had been forced by Donny's ruthless placement to go to the other end of the table; and a relatively famous hairdresser who for some reason had been allowed to sit with his girlfriend, a model.

'Don't quite know how to introduce Sophie these days,' said Donny. 'She used to be quite fun years ago, but then she went to work for a merchant bank –'

'American bank.'

'Even worse,' he continued. 'She bored everyone for years with her talk about Eurobonds and Third World debt. Then just when one had a bit of money and was looking for a friendly tip on the futures market, or an insider nod on an option or two, Sophie ups and leaves. No use to anyone at all. Then we hear she's become a secretary. It's a wonder she still gets invited round here at all.' He winked and sauntered off back to his end of the table.

He was joking, but there was a slightly uncomfortable element of reproach in his remarks. I have found that some of my so-called friends are genuinely horrified at the backward step in my career. At Cambridge your identity was tied up in your activities, like rowing or acting, and to a small extent, your subject. Since leaving, people have become more and more interested in what you do and less and less in what you think. Donny has become 'an interior designer', Dan is a 'writer'. I had been just about acceptable as a banker: the job itself frowned upon, the salary envied. As a secretary people simply do not know quite what to make of me. I have to make more of an effort to be included in any conversation, because my job is not a fit subject for discussion.

I observed my fellow guests. The literary editor was practically creaming himself on his exclusive presence at the paperback auction of Dan's novel. Dan is naturally diffident and was finding the whole performance rather tiresome, I thought.

'So rare to find such an international novel emanating from the pen of an Englishman.'

'Thank you. I'm Scottish really, but it doesn't matter.'

'Scottish? Fascinating ... Quite, quite ... I think I have some Scottish blood somewhere myself.'

'Really?'

I had taken a long gulp of Kir and felt obliged to help Dan out.

'Which paper are you from?' I asked.

He told me.

'Wasn't that the one that described Dan's book as a gay *Love Story* without the story?'

He glared at me.

Dan smiled. 'Oh, I quite liked that one,' he said. 'It enabled us to put "a gay *Love Story*" as a quote right across the front of the American edition.' He got up because the phone was ringing once again.

The first course was home-made pasta cooked exactly *al dente* and adorned with a little melted butter and a few shavings of white truffle. We were all concentrating so hard on rolling our tagliarini using only a fork that the conversation lapsed until our plates were swept away by the exquisitely handsome Cuban butler they had hired for the evening.

'Half a million, and its still only four o'clock in the afternoon, their time,' said Dan as he came back. 'I only get half of it, because of the split with my publisher, but it's still quite a lot.'

'We're talking telephone numbers,' Donny called from the other end of the table. 'Well, not London of course, but if you lived in the provinces.'

'It feels vaguely unreal,' said Dan, and poured some claret into everyone's glasses.

The conversation turned to money and we all took

turns to say what we would do if we were to receive a million pounds by chance. Apart from the dentist, it crossed no one's mind to give a penny of it away, to charities or good causes of any description. Several people said vaguely that it wouldn't be enough. The literary editor started his list with a Ferrari, but quickly changed his mind to an island when he noticed everybody yawning exaggeratedly at him. The model said that a million wouldn't buy you much of an island these days, unless he was thinking, she said, of a little atoll off the coast of his native land.

'What?'

'Scotland,' she said. 'You just told us you came from Scotland. I expect you could get a rock up there for a million.' It was the only thing she had said so far, but it was exquisitely well timed. I exchanged glances with her.

'And you, Sophie. It was Sophie, wasn't it?' said the literary editor. 'Would you give up being a secretary?'

'As a matter of fact, I'm not sure,' I replied. 'I've had rather an eventful time over the last few weeks.'

'Really?' he said.

'Oh yes, it's been a non-stop voyage of discovery . . . from the Pinters of the future to the occasional dead body.'

Conversation up and down the table had quietened with the mention of Pinter and came to a standstill with dead body. I instantly regretted saying it. The literary editor was being so condescending that I had felt obliged to overturn his assumptions, but I had gone too far. One day I hope I'll feel secure or mature enough to resist the temptation to shock people who patronize me. I looked up the table. Twenty faces were waiting for me to continue. I explained as briefly as I could. Several people had heard of Agatha, or had read the obituaries. I tried to turn the conversation around to the collection of anecdotes I had amassed about the world of theatre and film, but tonight they weren't tripping off my tongue with their usual fluency and I felt horribly glib.

The second course of roasted red peppers and aubergines with a pesto of fresh coriander arrived and I was saved from continuing by another telephone call from the States. Dan was away from the table for quite a while, and when we finished eating several people got up and changed places.

'Are you OK?' Anna, the dentist, interrupted whatever train of thought I had been immersed in. I had been finding it very difficult to concentrate.

'Yes, thanks ... Actually, no, I'm not. I probably shouldn't have come tonight. I'm not on very good form.'

'It must have been horrible for you ... Had she been ill for a long time?'

'Well, she had been off work with flu. I suppose she must have been very depressed ... It was suicide, you see.'

'Oh, how awful.'

'A massive overdose, they think.'

Anna rested her hand on my arm and we sat for a few moments in silence. I thought what a kind dentist she must be and imagined her being able to calm down the most recalcitrant child with her peaceful presence. She seemed to be debating internally whether to continue with the subject. Eventually she said, 'I think death must be something we get used to as we grow older, but the first time we experience it, it's terribly difficult.'

She described how her mother had died when she was a teenager. I was moved by the honesty of her description and recognized some of the symptoms I had been suffering, in a much more minor way. Then she said, 'A couple of months ago one of my patients died. She was only young – in her thirties – and I have found it very difficult to come to terms with. You see, she had a bad cold, or flu, or something, and she had just had her wisdom teeth out. I had prescribed her painkillers, and what seems to have happened is that she took them, but was also taking cold remedies – you know, those lemon drinks and that green syrup at night? All the medicines contained paracetamol, you see, and people don't realize how powerful it is. She lived on her own, and I think she can't have taken much notice of the warnings on the packet about the doses. When her boyfriend hadn't heard from her for a few days, he went round and found her in a coma. They got her to hospital, but her liver was irreparably damaged. There was nothing anybody could do, and she died.'

'God, how terrible,' I said. It seemed a woefully inadequate thing to say, and I wished, not for the first time, that there existed a better vocabulary of condolence. I held her hand for a moment or two. Her eyes had filled with tears, which I knew were not of sorrow but of anger at her inability to change events. I had spent the last week agonizing about the phone call I had had with Agatha. If only I had gone round then, rather than waiting until the next day. I found tears coming to my eyes.

'I think I could have saved her, you see,' I said, beginning to cry.

Anna put her arm round me.

'I doubt it very much. Once the damage is done to the liver, there's not much hope, I'm afraid.'

Somehow that opinion, coming from someone in the medical profession, consoled me a little.

The model had been half listening to what we were saying.

'Wasn't there something about that in the papers the other day? Apparently a consumer group is pressing for better labelling on those seemingly harmless cold preparations.'

'The thing is, they are harmless, if you take the right dosage, but you don't need very much more and then they're lethal.'

Donny had sensed the prevailing gloom at our end of the table and insisted on separating us. I went to congratulate Dan, who was sitting on his own, unable to take in the fact that he was about to be the recipient of nearly half a million dollars. The American paperback sale had reached $900,000, which was a record for an English (or Scottish) first novel.

Some of the guests started playing another dinner-party game, taking turns to say who they would kill on a whim if they had the power. It's a game, I'm somewhat ashamed to say, I've played at other dinner parties and enjoyed tremendously. Normally the first victims are the great and the good and the fun is in being more outrageously politically incorrect than the last person.

'Terry Waite,' suggested the hairdresser, to a round of applause.

I didn't have the stomach to join in. My mind was trying to take in what Anna had been saying. Could the same thing that had happened to Anna's patient have happened to Agatha? She had had a bad cold. She also drank a lot normally, and probably more when she was in pain. Didn't alcohol damage your liver too? I wondered if anyone had thought of the possibility of her death being an accident. At first the idea made me feel relieved, and then I realized with horror that it was perhaps even more tragic if it had been an accident. At least if she had committed suicide she had done so of her own free will. If it had been an accident . . .

'The Prince and Princess of Wales!' said another guest.

'Boring!' cried the rest.

'Oh, all right, Mother Teresa.'

'We've had her.'

The party was getting more and more rowdy, aided by a crate of champagne that had materialized when the conclusion of Dan's sale had been announced. I knew that at any minute Donny would force us to divide into two teams and play charades. I decided to go home.

I managed to pick up a taxi at Holland Park Avenue and, as it roared off, I stared out of the window. The taxi took the back route down Westbourne Grove, which was still alive with people eating kebabs. I saw a couple coming out of Khan's arm in arm, as Greg and I had done the other day. I felt strangely distant from them all. My brain kept running and rerunning Agatha's last few days.

As the taxi raced past Paddington Green Police Station my mind seemed to clear, like an epiphany. I sat up from my slouched position and gasped at the clarity of the thought. A rogue piece of the mental jigsaw suddenly slotted into place. Agatha's death couldn't have been an accident, because Agatha didn't approve of medicine. She was as likely to have a bottle of paracetamol in her bathroom cabinet as she was to have an espresso machine in her kitchen. Coffee was poison, I had often heard her say, and I knew that she felt just the same way about aspirin, or any other drug that normal people take to get them through minor ailments. I realized too that one of the reasons I had initially found it difficult to accept the premiss that she had killed herself was not just that I didn't want to accept it, but that I had never been able to envisage her actually swallowing an overdose of painkillers, because I couldn't imagine her having painkillers in her home.

The relief I felt at finally understanding something was instantly replaced by a creeping sensation of horror. So what had happened? If, as I thought, it wasn't suicide, and it couldn't have been an accident, the inescapable conclusion was that someone had given Agatha painkillers without her knowledge. Which meant that Agatha had been murdered.

19

Martin was not exactly pleased to be woken up, and from his tone of voice I rather thought that he wasn't exactly alone in bed either. He was especially irritated when he heard why I was ringing.

'Sophie, to be quite honest, I think that you ought to see a doctor. You're being irrational now. It's understandable, but you've got to get over this.'

'But just listen a minute –'

'No, I won't. And no, you mustn't go to the funeral. It's none of your business anyway.'

'Well, I bloody well found her, so it is my business . . . If the police are thinking the same as me, I'm probably a suspect.'

'You're really in fantasy-land now, Soph. Go to bed and in the morning go to the doctor. I think you do need some counselling, or something. I'll talk to you soon.' He put down the phone.

I wondered briefly whether he was right. I had not been feeling at all normal since the weekend and the theory I had worked out about Agatha's death did seem rather extreme. Martin was normally a great conspiracy theorist, and we used to spend hours discussing intrigues at the bank together. It wouldn't be like him to dismiss out of hand any idea he thought had an inkling of plausibility. I resolved to try to sleep and see how I felt in the morning before making any decision about what to do.

*

The cab dropped me outside the forbidding frontage of Golders Green crematorium. There were several dark-red brick buildings that looked like a smaller, sinister version of St Pancras Station. I stood in the pouring rain wondering where the funeral was. Eventually I noticed, on the other side of the forecourt, a door that said 'Reception'.

A surprisingly jolly man dressed in a black overcoat looked at his list and informed me that the funeral would be conducted in the East Chapel. He then offered to escort me there under the shelter of his large black umbrella. He told me that the smaller Bedford Chapel was hardly used these days, as there wasn't enough room in front for the cars to turn round, and I was relieved that I had stopped my cab from driving through the gates and clogging up the system. It wouldn't have been so bad if it had been a black cab, but it was one of those which had been painted like a newspaper to advertise the *Evening Standard*.

In the quiet of the chapel I was painfully aware of the sound of water dripping from my coat. I sat down several rows back to leave room for relatives. In the front pew stood Dorothy, and next to her a much older woman, who appeared a bit senile. In the row behind sat Anthony, several yards to the right of the women, and more or less in front of me. He hadn't appeared to notice my entrance. The vicar approached Dorothy and mumbled something to her. She nodded. Then she helped the old lady to her feet and what sounded like a tape-recorder started playing a piece of Bach I couldn't place. Four undertakers marched slowly in, carrying the coffin, and placed it on the catafalque. Anthony and I jumped to our feet, realizing at the same moment that we were the only other mourners. I can't remember much of what the vicar said. I remember thinking it terribly bland. He obviously had no idea who the deceased was. The old lady butted in, in quite a loud voice, at one point, 'Is she in that box over there?'

'Yes. She is,' Dorothy replied quietly, and gripped the old woman's arm.

'Oh, dear me, I don't like the look of that at all,' she said, and then fell silent again.

Then the tape clicked back on to play some unrecognizable hymn, the doors behind the coffin opened and it was cranked out of sight. I could only seem to think about how small the coffin was and how large and empty the chapel. It was like a small Victorian church, but there were no religious images of any description. I guessed it would have seated nearly a hundred people. For the first time in her life, I thought, and sniffed, Agatha's presence failed to fill the room.

The vicar indicated that we should leave. I suppose he didn't want us getting mixed up with the next funeral. I had noticed hearses circling the area as I arrived. It was a bit like stacking at Heathrow Airport. There were obviously fixed quarter-of-an-hour slots, with rigorous traffic control.

Dorothy helped the old woman towards the door. She was wearing the same long black coat as she had been at the hospital, almost as if she had known, I thought.

Anthony didn't move until they were outside. I followed him. There was a cloister behind the chapels where the flowers of the day had been placed under a name plaque of the deceased. There was practically a florist's shop under Agatha's name, including a huge cross made of white roses and an awful arrangement of purple chrysanthemums spelling the word MUM. Dorothy, seeing immediately that there had been a confusion, marched straight up to the wall, unslotted the plaque and swapped it with the one under the next arch. The much-loved mother had been called Margaret Brown. It was a trivial enough mistake, but it made me cry for the first time that day, especially since the contrast in floral tributes was so marked. Under Agatha's name now rested the small but beautifully tasteful arrangement of violets, wild flowers and herbs which had been on top of the coffin, and beside that a single deep velvety-red rose, with a small card attached, its message face-down. I thought it would be impertinent to stoop down to read what it said, although I longed to know who had sent such an unusual tribute.

The four of us stood as far apart from each other as we could, looking at the flowers. The old lady started muttering something, then looked at Anthony and said, 'Oh, dear, you have got old.' Dorothy drew her back sharply.

Then Anthony took a decisive step away. I hadn't really been able to see his face yet that day, but I caught a glimpse of it as he walked away. It was red and swollen from crying. He clutched a large handkerchief in one hand, but seemed unaware that his nose was running. I let him get several steps ahead, then followed. Dorothy had not exchanged a glance with me throughout. As I left the crematorium grounds, I looked back and saw her helping the old lady into the funeral car. They drove past me, two tiny faces floating in the back of a large limousine.

The whole ceremony had taken just under fifteen minutes. I wished with hindsight that I had kept the taxi, since it was raining just as hard and I had no idea where I was. I chose to turn left and started walking, hoping to come upon a bus stop or tube sooner or later.

Martin had been right about one thing. I shouldn't

have gone. It was a pathetically dingy exit for someone as colourful as Agatha. I was beginning to feel extremely resentful towards Dorothy. However bad her feud with Agatha might have been, I felt that it was churlish to have given her such a poor send-off. Unless . . . unless it was a deliberately low-key send-off, designed to attract as little attention as possible. I remembered my conversation with Dorothy the day before, if you could call those few terse, rude words a conversation. Why had she been so obstructive, I wondered. She, as far as I knew, had been the last person to see Agatha conscious on the Wednesday, after I left. Could they have argued again? Despite Martin's ridicule, I hadn't woken up entirely disposed to reject the conclusion that had seemed so clear the night before. As I stomped through the puddles, I wondered what, if anything, I should do about it.

Eventually I found the tube station and got the Northern Line to Leicester Square. It had stopped raining by the time I arrived at work, but I was still wet and cold. Anthony had not arrived and Janet was panting for a moment-by-moment account of the funeral.

'Oh, give me a break, for God's sake!' I snapped, and took the post into Agatha's room to open it. Several items in the mail required Agatha's signature and I was beginning to despair at the lack of guidance Anthony was providing. He hadn't been in the office since Tuesday. He had seemed to want me to stay on, then, and yet there wasn't much I could do without his authorization. Unattended post was piling up on Agatha's desk and I hated the lack of professionalism in failing to deal with it. I would have tendered my resignation that day, if there had been anyone in charge to tender it to.

I tore open a thick cream envelope, thinking as I did that the typeface looked familiar. Inside there was one sheet of vellum. It said, 'REMEMBER THE DAY OF THE JACKAL' and nothing more.

I remembered the note that had arrived a few days before and extricated it from the pile on the desk. The two typefaces were the same, and there had been a third before. I couldn't remember what it had said exactly, but the messages were beginning to look very threatening. I shivered. I had never seen a poison-pen letter before. I thought that they existed only in films and detective novels. I tried to remember what happened in *Day of the Jackal*. There was an assassination attempt on the French president, I thought. I couldn't remember whether it had been successful or not. It was a long time since I had seen the film.

I walked round the room, trying to decide what to do. A woman had died in circumstances that seemed suspicious to me, and she had received three threatening notes. I had been wondering all morning whether to get in touch with Mr Middlemarch and tell him about my unformed suspicions, but had stopped myself. Now I was beginning to feel that it was my duty to ring him. Not to do so would be withholding evidence. He had presented me with his card before he interviewed me. I found it in the back of my Filofax and rang the number nervously.

I think my explanation must have sounded rather peculiar. Mr Middlemarch interrupted on several occasions to say that he was perfectly satisfied that there was nothing suspicious. But I persisted in a garbled way and in the end, more out of courtesy than interest, I felt, he agreed to send someone round. It was nearly five o'clock and Janet was gathering up her things to leave when the uniformed officer arrived. I had decided not to discuss my theory with her. If I was right about Agatha's death, it was imperative that I told no one I didn't entirely trust. If I was wrong, I couldn't bear the prospect of her teasing. I had thought that Mr Middlemarch would be sensible enough to send someone round in plain clothes who would ask for me by name and hence avoid arousing Janet's interest. As it was, she put her head around the door and announced, 'PC Briggs to see you, Sophie.'

He was an extremely handsome policeman, with a thatch of thick corn-coloured hair and large, grinning white teeth. His appearance, together with her own natural nosiness, was enough to make Janet put her raincoat back on its hanger and hover around the door, pretending to tidy up. I started telling PC Briggs about my theory in a low voice. He didn't seem particularly interested, but he took the odd note or two.

'My information is,' he interrupted finally, 'that you are in receipt of some evidence pertaining to the inquiry.'

'Well, yes, I was just coming to that. You see, I didn't tell her when she rang because she seemed so cheerful that day –'

'Yes, yes. If I could just have a look at the evidence.'

I showed them to him.

'This one arrived last Thursday you see . . . and this one today.'

'But the deceased died on Sunday, am I right?'

'Yes,' I said impatiently.

'Well, I don't see the logic then,' he retorted.

'What do you mean?'

'Well, if, as you seem to think, someone is responsible for the deceased's demise, doesn't it seem rather peculiar that they would deliver a threatening letter five days after the death?'

'Oh.' That hadn't occurred to me. I wished I had

thought longer and harder before ringing Mr Middlemarch.

'Could I take a look, officer?' asked Janet, walking into the room.

'I don't see why not,' he said, and handed them to her.

A huge smile lit her face as she read.

'Oh, not him again!'

'You know who wrote these?' I was astonished.

'I do. I'm surprised you haven't come across the file. His name's Watt, but we file him under Weirdo. He's this barmy writer who keeps trying to get Agatha to take him on,' she explained. 'He's always sending in new plays or stories, and they are absolutely awful. I mean, officer, I don't know much about literature, but I've read some of them and they're a standing joke with Viv and me. Agatha always turns him down with the standard letter about being too busy, you know, but he just won't take no for an answer. Then one day, she gets so sick of him that she writes saying that he has absolutely no talent and that she would bet her last pound that he will never be published or performed . . . Well, after that the notes started arriving. They're always one-liners, very often referring to an author who was rejected but then became famous . . . Hang on a minute, I'll get the file.'

I could feel myself going pinker and pinker. PC Briggs was trying to keep a straight face.

'Here, now, look, in July he must have discovered that James Joyce was rejected, because we have "REMEMBER ULYSSES!" There are several others . . .' She offered the file to PC Briggs, who took a quick look and then handed it to me. I looked. The typeface and paper were always the same. I have never felt more embarrassed.

'Well, that seems to answer that,' said the policeman.

'Look, I am terribly sorry,' I stammered.

'Not to worry at all, young lady.'

I resented this from someone who was obviously younger than me, but resisted saying so. He told me that death was often difficult to come to terms with, and asked if I had thought about ringing the Samaritans. I said that I wasn't thinking of killing myself, but he explained that they offered a bereavement counselling service. I thanked him for his concern.

'*Day of the Jackal* was rejected about seventeen times, I think,' added Janet as she escorted PC Briggs out of the office.

'Really? It must be a funny business, this. That's a great film, that is.'

20

I spent Friday evening in a state of fury with myself. What annoyed me most was that I had now lost all credibility with the police. If there were something funny about Agatha's death, I would hardly be able to persuade them to investigate it now. I wished that I had thought logically about the stupid notes.

I decided to plot Agatha's last days scientifically, charting all the facts I knew in a diagram. I found some felt-tip pens and a ruler and divided a sheet of paper into five equal divisions and headed them with the days of the week.

In Wednesday's space I put my name, and after it Dorothy's. Thursday and Friday were blank. I appeared in brackets, signifying the phone call on Saturday, then on Sunday again. All I knew otherwise was that three bottles of whisky had been consumed, the kitchen cleaned and the cat let out. It wasn't much to go on. Perhaps I was being paranoid after all.

I didn't feel like seeing anyone on Saturday. I wanted some time on my own to clear my head, or at least fill it with different images. I went to Leicester Square, ate huge amounts of dim sum and, with the aid of *Time Out*, found four films I wanted to see, synchronized their performance times and moved from one screen to another for the rest of the day. The last was a midnight presentation of a film about a ghost who comes back in order to find his own murderer. That was a mistake. When I got home I went to bed and dreamt that Agatha was negotiating a contract for her own death and standing behind me while I typed it on a manual machine. I woke up agitated and picked up the phone, half expecting to have to continue with the dictation.

'Sorry to call so early, but we've just got in and we're going to bed now so I thought I'd just let you know we were home.'

'Mum!'

'Oh, we've had a lovely time, but the plane was delayed and we seem to have been travelling for hours ... Hang on ... Reg says we have been travelling for hours!'

'I'm so glad to hear you.'

'I thought you might be worried.'

'No, I mean, yes.' What with one thing and another, I had completely forgotten that they were coming home late on Saturday night and it hadn't crossed my mind to wonder why they hadn't called.

'Why don't you come for dinner tonight. There's lots of stuff in the freezer, and we can show off our tans before they fade.'

I said I'd love to and agreed to arrive at about seven.

I love the walk from Pinner Station to my mother's house. There's something very comforting about the high street with its little shops and restaurants lovingly preserved, their windows lit with modest Christmas decorations. Even the entrance to Sainsbury's is disguised so that a passing traveller would have no idea that a huge supermarket lurks behind. I bought a bottle of the kind of sweet German wine my mother prefers in the off-licence, and the owner greeted me warmly, remembering, no doubt, all the money my schoolfriends and I used to spend on sweets, and later cigarettes, in his shop.

'You've had your hair cut,' he said, as if surprised that I had changed at all from the fifteen-year-old in long socks and plaits that he used to serve. 'Makes a nice change, although you look a lot different from your mother like that.'

I knew that this was not a compliment, but thanked him all the same.

I continued up past the church and turned into our street. Like me, my mother was an only child. Her parents died in a car crash when I was a baby, which must have been devastating for her, since they had always been very close, even when she married my father, whom they didn't consider worthy of their beautiful daughter. Even if they had lived, I suppose that we would have moved back to their house when my father left us, since the flat near the Portobello Road was rented. As it was, the house was standing empty as if waiting for us when we moved in. It was ages before my mother got up the courage to redecorate, but when she finally did it was at the height of Laura Ashley mania and she made the house very pretty, in a feminine kind of way, with lots of pinks and yellows and a country-style kitchen complete with an Aga, which I have always found incongruous in what is, essentially, a 1930s suburban villa.

Reg is a permanent fixture in my mother's life and they do everything together, but he has never technically moved in. He has a house of his own in Hatch End, although he doesn't seem to spend much time there. I think my mother has always been afraid to share her life completely with another man and that is her safety valve. She met him when she was still married, because he was the surveyor who valued the house for probate when her parents died. She always says that she was so upset at the time she didn't notice him, but he obviously fell in love at first sight and as soon as we moved back to Pinner he came courting. Because she is so pretty, my mother is used to having things done for her, and because Reg volunteered his services, he was used quite ruthlessly as a garden-digger and general factotum. I don't think it occurred to my mother for years that he was interested in her, or maybe it did and she is less green than she is cabbage-looking (a favourite expression of Reg).

I think that Reg would have liked nothing more than to marry my mother and have some children. But my mother has always resisted. Having survived the trauma of a broken marriage and being orphaned at around about the same time, she managed to organize her life exactly as she wanted it, and didn't want anything, or anybody, to interfere with her security again. Luckily for me, Reg stuck around anyway. He has always been the kindest of stepfather figures and, even though our tastes and politics are very different, we generally get along well.

I rang the door bell and cringed. A few Christmases ago Reg bought my mother a door bell capable of playing ninety-nine different tunes. They had it programmed to chime the first seven notes of 'Una Paloma Blanca' today. Mum opened the door and gave me a great hug and a kiss.

'Do you have to have that awful tune on?' I said.

'Well, it's to keep us in the holiday spirit.'

'But isn't that a Spanish song? Madeira's Portuguese, isn't it?'

'Oh, I don't know,' she said. 'They played it all the time in the night-club at the hotel, didn't they, Reg?

Anyway –' she lowered her voice – 'it's better than Christmas carols, which is what he wanted on.'

'But it's only half-way through November!' I said.

'Quite. So stop complaining,' she said, and winked at me.

Her long, wavy hair was even fairer than usual, with natural highlights from the sun. Unlike most women of her age, my mother doesn't like to sunbathe and so her skin has not aged much, but she had still managed to pick up a light-golden tan that made her eyes seem bluer than ever. She was wearing a simple navy linen shift, obviously a new and expensive purchase, and quite unsuitable for a cold November evening, but she looked lovely in it. I looked at my own black jeans and big Aran jumper and wished I had made more of an effort. Reg was in the kitchen, wearing a plastic apron with the Martini label printed on it and stirring some soup on the top of the Aga. He offered me a glass of Madeira with ice, claiming that this was the fashionable way to drink it, and we sat down to eat, almost immediately.

They were very eager to give me a blow-by-blow account of their splendid holiday and I ate two delicious courses without saying anything except an occasional murmur in appreciation of the food. My mother had recently taken a cordon bleu cookery course, and we were eating the dishes she had prepared and frozen. A shiny, clear consommé, followed by Bœuf Bourguignonne. The meal was let down only by the vegetables – plain frozen peas, with no attempt at disguise.

'But, Soph, you should go yourself. You'd love it there,' said Reg. 'Go on, let's book you a week away. I'll pay! It'll be a kind of early Christmas present. She's looking a bit peaky, don't you think, darling?'

'She doesn't take care of herself,' added my mother.

'She does,' I said wearily. 'It's just that she hasn't had such a brilliant week.'

'Oh, I'm sorry, darling. We've been going on and on.'

'No, no, really. It was fascinating . . . It's just that —' I began to explain.

They were as shocked as I had expected them to be, and as sympathetic. My mother let me blub all over her new dress and Reg rushed around trying to find me some brandy. I even managed to tell them about the incident with PC Briggs and they assured me that they would have done the same thing in the circumstances. I explained the accident versus suicide arguments and my mother said that she had read an article about paracetamol recently herself. I omitted to tell them that I hadn't altogether ruled out my own theory. I didn't want to hear that I was being silly again.

Whether it was because he sensed that I would like to be alone with my mother or because *Inspector Morse* was about to begin, Reg left us to do the dishes together and went into the front room to watch television. My mother washed and I dried in silence for a while.

'I feel awful that I was so horrible about Agatha Brown when we spoke the other day,' my mother finally said.

'Well, I've been wanting to ask you about that,' I responded. 'You see, since her death I've been having trouble trying to formulate a picture of her. There seem to be so many contradictions. Why did you dislike her?'

I didn't think that I would get a satisfactory answer from my mother. She seemed to be thinking about her response for a long time before she spoke, but she must have realized that an answer was important to me, because she very nervously began to tell her story.

'Nobody seemed to know where those two girls came

from,' she began, 'and they were quite a daunting pair, I can tell you. Agatha, if that was her name, was always the dominant one. Dorothy was a bit younger, I think, and hero-worshipped her sister. They always seemed to be the first people to know things. Like what to wear, what was fashionable, that kind of thing. They claimed that they had seen the Beatles in the Cavern, for instance, although i never believed half of what they said. Marcus used to say that I was jealous, because they were so much more intelligent than me. I don't know why I stood for that kind of talk then. You certainly wouldn't, would you? They looked very similar, except that Dorothy was beautiful and somehow Agatha just wasn't. She was very attractive to men, though. I'm sure that she had had an affair with Marcus, although he would never say. He said it was too bourgeois of me to ask. She used to dismiss me too. If ever I tried to talk to her at a party she would look right over my shoulder and, as soon as somebody more interesting crossed her path of vision, she would be off. Often when I was in mid-sentence. They didn't think that I had a proper job and, even though they were always talking about what they did, if I ever told them about my day, they would exchange glances and laugh.'

The picture she was painting was almost exactly as I had imagined it when Agatha had described those times. I felt a great surge of love for my mother, who would never understand (and why should she?) that working as a waitress in a Soho coffee bar was probably not a topic of conversation for the chattering classes, whereas being a theatrical agent was.

'Do you remember anyone else from that crowd?' I asked.

'Well, it always varied, you see. They were very popular, knew ever so many people, although I always thought it was a bit superficial. They weren't really like friends, if you know what I mean. Agatha always had a different man. Often several different ones in an evening. There was one guy who used to be quite a regular. Can't remember his name. Marcus always called him the bookie, because that's what he looked like. We could never see what they saw in him –'

'Was it Jack?'

'No, I don't think so. He was the handsome one who went off with her sister, wasn't he? No, he was quite nice to me when I met him once. He wasn't snobby, more normal. No, the bookie was called something like Terry, something like that ... What got me was all their airs and graces. Marcus told me that it was all a sham anyway, because they weren't really upper class, like they pretended, but actually quite common –'

When my mother says the word common, she purses her lips afterwards. It is one of the most pejorative words in the Pinner vocabulary. I remembered that it was a word that had flown through my mind at the funeral when the old lady accompanying Dorothy had spoken. Her voice had quite a strong London accent, which had surprised me, since it didn't fit with the voices of Dorothy or Agatha. I wondered again who she was.

'He seemed to think that was a good laugh.' She finished rinsing the last saucepan. 'Would you like a cup of tea?'

I said I'd love one. From her description I could see why my mother didn't like Agatha, but I felt that what she had told me hardly justified the strength of emotion in her voice the other day on the phone. She was holding something back.

'I shouldn't go on, though,' said Mum. 'I mean, the poor woman. Nobody would wish that on her.'

I realized that she felt the conversation was now closed, but I was determined to press on. 'Why did you stop seeing them?' I said.

'Oh, I suppose that you came along and we drifted apart.' Almost the same words as Agatha had used. I believed them as much now as I had then.

'Did my father see her again?' I asked, almost fearing that the answer would be affirmative.

'Oh no. Absolutely not. It was really his decision not to. He felt very strongly about it. I can't say I minded though . . .' She trailed off, realizing that she had rather blown her cover. I was looking straight at her. 'Well, I suppose there's no harm in telling you now. I wouldn't have done before, but since the poor woman's dead – '

'What?'

'Well, as you probably have worked out, I was pregnant a little bit before your father and I married.'

'I had worked that out, yes.'

'We were delighted, though. I had always wanted a baby and Marcus was pleased as anything. We didn't tell anyone for a while, and I was very slim in those days and I didn't show. One evening we were all out together, except that Marcus was late. I couldn't drink alcohol, because it made me feel sick when I was pregnant, and Agatha kept joking about me. I was so fed up that I whispered to her why I couldn't drink. I think she must have thought that I was telling her something secret, although she would have been the last person I would confide in, but I wasn't, I was just whispering so that the others wouldn't hear because we hadn't really decided to tell anyone yet. Well, she took me on one side and told me that I mustn't think of having the baby. It would hold Marcus back in his career, I was too young, too irresponsible, and too stupid. Couldn't I see that it was only a passing infatuation for Marcus? She went on and on at me, and then started insisting that I go with her the next day to an abortionist. It was horrible. She even offered to pay for it. I kept telling her that we wanted the baby, but she wouldn't listen. By the time Marcus arrived, I was in floods and floods of tears and quite hysterical. When he asked what had been going on, I was so upset I couldn't tell him. She obviously thought that I hadn't told him I was pregnant. I said to Marcus, "Just take me home", and he did. And when I calmed down I told him. He was outraged. I've never seen him so angry. I thought he would kill her. I managed to persuade him that I was all right and we decided that we wouldn't mix with that crowd any more. And that was the last time I saw her. I'm sure it was the last time Marcus saw her too. You see, he loved the idea of you. He loved you very much. He just wasn't able to cope with the responsibility of a family very well. And, of course, in some ways that cow was right, because I was too ordinary for him . . . Well, you did ask, Sophie,' she said, seeing that tears were coursing down my cheeks.

I think that I was crying more at the thought of my father wanting me than at Agatha's attempt to get rid of me. I had always assumed that I was a complete accident and my father hadn't wanted me at all, but that he had, rather nobly, put up with me for a while when I arrived. For the first time in my adult life I felt I needed to know my father. Perhaps, I thought, he sometimes thinks about me and wonders what I am like. But I couldn't talk about this to my mother, because Reg came back into the kitchen, and I knew it would hurt his feelings tremendously if I expressed what I was thinking.

21

Reg offered to drive me home, but I declined. I wanted to spend some time on my own thinking about everything that had been said. I wasn't sure that he should be driving anyway, since he was well over half-way down the bottle of Madeira. In the end we compromised and he drove me the short distance to Harrow-on-the-Hill Station, which is a main junction.

The Metropolitan Line rattled its way to Finchley Road. I stared out of the window, mesmerized by the passing lights and deep in thought. The train came to a standstill, for no apparent reason, just past Neasden. I found myself gazing across the tracks and down into someone's back room. The television was on. I could see a brightly lit box in the corner of the window; a woman came into the room with a tray and was about to sit down when she must have realized the curtains were open. She put the tray down and went to close them. For a second her face appeared at the window and looked out into the darkness, then, with a sudden movement, the curtains were drawn and the little world I had been looking at disappeared.

I thought how strange it was that all the rectangles of light in all the houses along the track contained lives and stories that I would never know. Sometimes the spaces we inhabit impinge upon each other for just a moment and then we separate off again in different directions. I wondered absently whether I had any connection with the person who had just drawn her curtains. If I were to meet her, how many hours would we spend talking before finding someone we knew in common? The enormity of life makes individuals so small they become almost invisible and yet there often seems to be an uncanny interconnection between us all. My past had collided long ago with Agatha's, and by chance our lives had collided again. Was this so strange, given that she and my parents were of similar age, had lived in the same city, at the same heady, communicative time, and had shared interests and beliefs? No. And yet, I thought, as the train started up again, if Agatha had had her way, I wouldn't have existed.

I wondered why I didn't feel any differently towards Agatha because of this. It didn't seem to have anything to do with me. I may have been literally the subject of a discussion, but nothing more than that. I couldn't feel angry with Agatha for advising abortion. Everything I knew about her indicated that she was a prototype feminist, which I admired. In her odd, bossy way, she was probably only trying to help. There are ways of saying things, however, and I felt she must have been a very cold person to have spoken to my mother like that. More importantly, it hadn't been any of her business. She obviously wanted to control everyone and everything around her. Which was fine for her job, but it didn't seem to have brought her much joy otherwise. The image of her lying in her grubby flat once again crossed my mind. Perhaps it was suicide, after all. It seemed the obvious way for someone who has to be in control to die. But no, the more I tried to convince myself that Agatha had killed herself, the less I was convinced.

I remembered watching her as she crossed Soho Square on the way in to the office one day in October. She was about twenty yards ahead of me, unaware that I was behind. It was a cold morning but the autumnal red of the trees seemed to glow as the first rays of sunshine broke through an almost smoky mist. Agatha was leaping from side to side, scrunching leaves with her boots like a child, obviously delighting at the sound they made. It was the action of a person who loved life.

There was a message on my answerphone from Martin when I got back. I decided that it was too late to call him back but I felt wide awake, so I started to tidy up the flat, which I had neglected all week. I threw away last week's Sunday papers, knowing that I would never read them now. I'm happy to say that I have grown out of the habit of keeping papers in the expectation that I will read them one day and cut out the articles that interest me. I did the washing up and hoovered the living room. One of the best things about not having any neighbours is that I can make as much noise as I like at whatever time of night. I take great pleasure in hoovering during the early hours of the morning; it's one of the ostensible signs of my freedom. Before I bought my flat in Primrose Hill, I used to live in a rented apartment in Belsize Park where my neighbours downstairs were so neurotic, and the sound-proofing so inadequate, they would complain if I went to the bathroom after midnight.

There was a huge heap of unwashed clothes in my bedroom which I set about sorting into two piles: one for the dry-cleaners and one to be service-washed. Underneath the last pair of leggings I discovered Agatha's portable dictaphone machine and a few documents. I couldn't think what they were doing there, but then I remembered picking them up in Agatha's flat after my ill-advised recce last Monday. Had that really been only less than a week ago? I had sat at work for what seemed like an age, complaining about not being able to get on with things because Anthony wasn't in, and all the time there had been a full twenty-minute tape languishing on my bedroom floor at home. I got out my briefcase, which I hadn't had a reason to use since leaving the bank, and put everything in. Then I took the white broderie anglaise sheets off my bed, trying not to think about the reason they had been on in the first place, and put them in the service-wash pile. I put plain navy percale sheets on the bed and laid some clothes for the morning over a chair. The colour I wear most often is black, but I was sick of its connotations after the last week, so I chose almost the opposite, a shell-pink bouclé suit with a collarless jacket and short skirt which had been Jerry's favourite, and, for that reason, hadn't been worn for ages. I couldn't resist trying it on again and, I have to admit, being rather pleased with myself for having lost weight around the waist.

Anthony raised his eyebrows when I walked in to the office, briefcase in hand and wearing my feminine but ever-so-expensive clothes. He was giving Janet dictation, but stopped, mid-sentence, and appraised me. I suppose that I must have looked a lot different from the dripping mass he had last encountered in the crematorium.

He did a wolf-whistle in appreciation. It was a crude gesture and even Janet looked surprised. He also did a double-take, as if his guard had slipped momentarily, and coughed falsely.

I said hallo in what I thought was a dignified way,

then put my briefcase down on my desk and proceeded to open the post. I wanted to look as efficient as I could after Friday's débâcle.

I sorted out the documents on which I needed Anthony's advice and took them in to him. He went through them with me and made some flattering remarks about how I had chosen to deal with various matters. Then he said, 'I gather from Janet that you called the police on Friday.'

'Yes. Sorry about that. I think it must have been stress. I was a bit mixed up and I put those two threatening notes together and made five!' I was squirming with embarrassment.

'The reason I ask,' he said, 'is that I have been having doubts myself.'

'Really?' I replied as nonchalantly as I could. 'What kind of doubts?'

'It occurs to me that maybe we have all been too hasty. You obviously have your doubts and now, even though I was convinced at first, I feel that her death is somewhat open to question. My theory is a little more boring than yours. There's no demented axe-murderer author in mine.' He winked at me patronizingly, 'I think it must have been an accident.'

'Whatever makes you say that?' I asked, affecting surprise.

'Apparently it isn't uncommon. I read something in the papers a while back.'

Why had everyone in the world seen this article apart from me?

'Wait a minute,' I said, pretending I didn't understand what he was talking about, 'You think that she accidentally overdosed?'

'It's a possibility, don't you think? After all, didn't you

say yourself that she had seemed cheerful when you last spoke to her?'

'When did you last speak to her?' I asked, trying to keep my voice as level as I could.

'Oh, Thursday, I think it was,' he said, looking, I felt, slightly uncomfortable.

'And she sounded?'

'Her usual self.'

'Well,' I said, 'perhaps you should tell Mr Middlemarch, if you're really convinced.'

'Oh, I have,' he said, rather throwing me off-balance.

I felt uneasy. Why was someone who had claimed to be saddened but not surprised by Agatha's suicide now suggesting that it was an accident? And why, if he had informed the Coroner of his doubts, was he telling me? I couldn't work it out. I spent the rest of the morning trying to put more data on to the computer, but my mind was whirring with hypotheses. In the end, I feigned a migraine and asked for the rest of the day off. Anthony readily agreed. He even offered to drive me home, but I declined vehemently, saying that I wanted to walk in the fresh air.

The taxi drew up outside the Italian off-licence and delicatessen opposite my flat and I decided to treat myself to a ciabatta roll with thick slices of home-cooked ham and beef tomato. I started eating it in the shop while I chatted to the owner and it was so delicious that I ordered another one immediately. The normally laconic man behind the food counter smiled as he sliced open another roll and ladled in the fresh mayonnaise. It was only when I got home that I realized I had flour all over my nose.

I ate the rest of my late lunch poring over my chart. I

added Anthony's name in brackets on Thursday. He and Dorothy were the obvious suspects. But why, if he had been instrumental in her death, was he now trying to change the supposed cause of death? If he were the killer, it would surely be more convenient for him if people believed that she had committed suicide. If he were now changing his view, wouldn't Mr Middlemarch become suspicious? Perhaps not. In my limited experience Mr Middlemarch wasn't a hugely imaginative man. I felt it would be easy enough to commit a less than perfect murder right under his officious nose.

I stared at my plan as if an answer would leap out at any moment. I toyed with the idea of ringing Martin and bamboozling him into discussing my theory, but I resisted. In the end, even I know where to draw the line. I was saved from further deliberations by Costas and Elena, his wife, who had finally paid off the loan on their washing machines and wanted to take me out to celebrate. As we ate kleftiko in the cousin's taverna, I realized that their motive for inviting me was less than pure, given that the object was to mollify me before the builders moved in to renovate, very noisily it turned out, the flat below mine, but we spent a jolly evening nevertheless and, after I don't know how many bottles of retsina, I felt emboldened to ask them their thoughts about murder. I was sure that I appeared to be posing an utterly objective question, from mere intellectual interest. The funny thing about alcohol is that when you are slightly drunk, you feel very drunk indeed; when you are half-way drunk, you know that you have drunk a little; but when you are absolutely pissed out of your head, you feel absolutely sober. Elena fell silent at that point, and I vaguely remember her looking at me in a worried kind of way, as she has done ever since. Costas, who was keen to round off the meal with several tumblers of Metaxa – one person needs one, how you say, digestive, to help with stomach after such a meal – warmed to the theme and gave me a short (or, maybe, quite extensive) lecture on Greek tragedy and the human impulse of revenge.

When I lay down to sleep (having constructed an assault course of chairs and saucepans from the double-locked door of my flat to my bed for any potential intruder), my head was swimming with stories of poisoned clothes and axes. The family, according to Costas, was an institution writhing with suppressed hatred, but the power of sexual magnet (as he called it) was even stronger. No wonder Elena, who presumably falls into both categories, was keen to bundle him off unceremoniously, rather than stay for the last nightcap Costas and I were intent on drinking.

22

The office appeared deserted when I arrived the next morning, which was a relief because I was suffering. It was ironic that having pretended to have a migraine the day before, I had now given myself one voluntarily. My brain kept throwing up sporadic recollections of the conversation with Costas and I almost smiled, but any movement of my head was painful. At first I thought I was the only one there, but after a while I began to distinguish the murmur of conversation coming from behind Anthony's closed door above the general city noise that seemed much louder today than it usually did.

I wanted to talk to Anthony. I had decided, whether it was wise or not, to confront him with the obvious question, 'If Agatha didn't take medicine, how could she have accidentally overdosed?'

I was beginning to think that my suspicions were becoming a bit obsessive and I wanted to clear up my nagging doubts. However, I didn't want to talk to him in front of Janet, so I decided to wait until they had finished whatever it was they were doing.

There were only three envelopes in the post. Two addressed to me were from clients asking for all their files to be transferred to their new agent. I swore, because one was from Mark Adams, an actor whose numerous voice-over contracts I had already painstakingly transferred to the computer. The third was an air-mail envelope containing another request from the Californian university for permission to produce *The Hairs in the Sink*. Their performance was just a month away and they were getting desperate. It was obvious that they had gone ahead rehearsing the play, assuming that permission would be forthcoming.

I looked through the entire pile of mail on Agatha's desk, before remembering that the last letter from them had been one of the things we had gone through at her flat. She had taken the letter from me, I'd assumed to give to Dorothy later that evening. I supposed that in the tragic events of the next week Dorothy and Jack had forgotten to deal with it. Given that they had been so rude to me on the phone the last time I had rung, I had half a mind to leave the matter, but the university drama department was persistent and I felt sure that, if I ignored this request, increasingly hysterical faxes would follow. I rang Dorothy's number. There was an answerphone. I left a message for Dorothy to call me urgently at work.

There wasn't much else for me to do. Anthony's door was still closed and I was loath to start putting more information on the computer until I had a better idea of the numbers of clients who had decided to stay with the agency, so I went into Agatha's office, retrieved Jack Burton's play from behind the cushion on the leopardskin sofa and began reading again.

Towards the end of the first act, it emerges that Sid, Jemima and Bella share a secret. Although in a subordinate role, Sid almost seems to be blackmailing the women with it. The moment when the audience thinks that they are about to hear what the secret is, Johnny walks on to the stage, the rest of the cast falls silent and the curtain comes down for the interval. The more I read of Jack Burton's play, the more I liked it, as much for the sharpness of the dialogue as for the glimpse it gave me of Agatha when young. It was clear that Jemima was based on Agatha and I thought that Bella must be Dorothy. Was Johnny Jack himself? It was like looking at a very stylized photograph of the trio when younger. I remembered that my mother had said that a man hung around with them a lot. What had my father called him? The bookie? Perhaps he was Sid in the play.

It must have been written before the falling-out, because Agatha ceased being his agent after that. I wondered when that had been. The copyright line in the book read 1962 and I imagined that it had been published to coincide with the West End run. How long after that had Dorothy and Agatha fallen out? I realized I could find out quite easily by looking up the files and, since I had little else to do, I took the key to the basement door from Agatha's desk and started walking down the stairs.

The cellar was much colder than it had been in September and I wished that I had put on my coat. The boxes were stacked four deep and the two I wanted access to were inevitably at the bottom of a stack. After a great deal of heaving and pushing, I managed to open the lid and I pulled out the file labelled Burton. There was quite a lot of correspondence. It was mostly requests from film companies for reading copies, and letters I couldn't understand in foreign languages, which I imagined must be from theatres abroad. I replaced the file and opened the box for 1963. There were fewer letters in this of the same sort and no evidence of any formal break between agent and playwright. I was just about to close the file and open the 1964 box when the light in the cellar went out. I gasped. In the split second before it had happened I had sensed someone standing at the top of the stairs watching me. I crouched petrified. There cannot have been more than a few seconds of silence, but my mind went into hyperdrive, working out my options. I knew that it would be no use screaming because it was too early in the day for the Chinese restaurant to be open. The ground floor of the building had been vacant for some weeks, the graphic design company who occupied it having gone bust. A scream in the streets of Soho would not seem odd to any passer-by.

Then suddenly the light came back on. Anthony White was standing at the top of the stairs.

'I am sorry. I was just going out and I saw the light on,' he said, starting down the stairs.

'Christ, you scared me!'

'Sorry. I didn't realize you were here.'

I was about to ask him why, in that case, he had turned the light back on, but my teeth were chattering.

'I'm glad I caught you, though,' he continued. 'Are you all right? You seem jumpy ... It's really that I wanted to talk to you about.'

'What?'

'Well, what with the migraines and everything. You were late in today and Janet said that you went home early the other day. I really think you need a rest, don't you? Through no fault of your own, you've become very involved in something that really shouldn't concern you. I'm not sure it's healthy for you to stay.'

'I'm fine,' I said, then realized that he wasn't asking me but telling me. 'You mean you want me to leave?'

'Well, it's really the last thing I need at this moment in time, but you're so pale and troubled. I couldn't take responsibility for damaging your health ... Don't worry about the money. I'm sure we can pay you till the end of the contract. What is it? Three weeks now?'

'That's very kind,' I stammered. I have never been

dismissed from a job. It was an awful feeling.

'Not at all,' he said, and turned to go. It was clear that the exchange was over.

'Do you mean now?' I said. 'Surely I should clear up the things on my desk?'

He hesitated for a minute.

'Well, if you're sure you want to. Very professional attitude. When you're better, you must feel you can give me as a reference.' He waited for me to replace the file, then he restacked the boxes and followed me upstairs. He seemed to have forgotten that he was on his way out when he had found me in the cellar.

It was obvious from Janet's expression of false pity and concern that she had known what was going to happen. They had probably been plotting it together earlier in his office. I ignored her offer to make me a cup of tea. I must have looked a ridiculous figure in my pink suit, which was covered in dust from the basement (my casual, more comfortable clothes were at that very moment swirling round in the free service-washes I had negotiated with Costas before I caught up with his tally of drinks the night before), stacking the papers on my desk into neater piles and signing off from the computer.

I had thought there would be more to do, but the clearing-up operation took approximately ten minutes. I went to the lavatory, took several deep breaths and came back determined to get out of the office, if not with dignity, then certainly without crying.

'Well, it's been nice knowing you,' I said, gritting my teeth.

'Hang on a minute,' said Janet, and reached to answer the phone. 'Brown and Brown, can I help you?' she chirruped in her usual manner, which today I found

unnecessarily triumphant. 'Yes? Yes? Oh, not again!'
She threw the phone back on to its rest.

'What?' I asked.

'That's been happening all morning. The phone rings
and it feels like there's someone at the other end, but
they don't say anything. Then they hang up . . . Haven't
you forgotten something, by the way?'

'What?'

'Your briefcase? It's sitting under your desk. You
wouldn't want to forget that.'

'Thank you,' I said, and picked it up. I had completely
forgotten Agatha's dictaphone machine and the twenty-
minute tape inside it, until I felt the weight of the
briefcase.

'Oh, there's this bloody tape,' I said, opening the case.

'I'll do it if you like.'

'No,' I replied. 'It's the least I can do.'

'Well, you're a real glutton for punishment,' Janet
sniped, quite offended that I had turned her offer down.
'I'm going out to lunch. I don't suppose you'll be here
when I get back, so I'll say goodbye now.'

'Yeah. Goodbye,' I said, without emotion.

'Good luck,' she added, giving me a perplexed look.

It was eerie hearing Agatha's very animated voice
through my headset. There was an odd gurgling sound
in the background, but her voice was as clear as a bell.
The first couple of letters were standard stuff – heavily
ironic persuasive notes about payments overdue and fine
contractual points. Then she spoke directly to me.

'I say, darling, you don't mind doing me a personal
one, do you. It's just that these damn banks have to have
everything in writing these days . . . Now, where is it?'

The background noise grew fainter and I realized that

Agatha must have been wandering around the flat looking for something.

'Yes, here we are . . . To the Manager, Barclays Bank, Regent Street – It's the one next to Liberty's, darling. Would you find out the proper address? Further to our telephone conversation of today – Put the date in, darling – I should like to confirm my instructions, colon, a standing order of £2,000 per month from my deposit account number — to current account number — full stop, new paragraph, or whatever looks neatest, darling. Yours ever, or whatever you say to a bank manager, darling, etc. Next, fax to Cormac's hotel. Dearest (or whatever I call him nowadays), so sorry I can't be there for the previews. Unusually for me, I have been rather poorly this last week, but I'm much recovered and – Darling, could you ring up and see if you could book a flight for the opening night? I usually travel British Airways, but, you know, I rather fancy trying Virgin . . . Where was I? I will try –' She stopped dictating at the sound of a buzzer – her entryphone, I assumed. There was silence for a few seconds, then Agatha's voice called out, 'I'll leave the door off the latch, let yourself in.' Then silence again apart from the faint noise in the background which had been there in varying degrees throughout.

I was about to play back the tape, thinking that it had ended, when I heard what sounded like a door slamming and footsteps.

'I was just about to have a bath and a cocktail, darling. I didn't expect you so soon,' said Agatha's voice, slightly muffled. She had obviously put the dictation machine down a few feet away from her.

'May I join you?'

And there the tape ran out.

23

I don't know how often I played back the tape hoping that I had misheard. I tried to convince myself that I couldn't possibly recognize from four monosyllabic words the owner of the voice that had spoken them. If it hadn't been such a distinctive voice, then perhaps I wouldn't have been so sure. I thought about erasing the tape and pretending that it didn't exist, but I knew that if I did I might start thinking that it was only a product of my overactive imagination. I was shaking as I took it out of the playback machine and put it into my handbag. I printed out the business letters and left them on Janet's desk. I printed a copy of the bank manager's letter and put that in my briefcase, then deleted the file from the computer. I didn't think that Agatha's personal finances were any business of Anthony or Janet. I hadn't bothered to type the unfinished fax to Cormac O'Hara, or the conversation that I had just overheard.

I had one last, swift look around Agatha's office and, just as I was turning to leave, I saw the slim Penguin paperback on the sofa. I picked up Jack Burton's play and put it in my briefcase.

I put my head round Anthony's door and said goodbye in as normal voice as I could. He looked up and waved pleasantly enough.

It was pouring with rain in the street below and I was soaking wet by the time I found a taxi. Once home, I walked straight to my table and stared at my plan. Then

I took a red felt-tip and wrote across Thursday and Friday in large capital letters GREG.

When he had told me he was seeing someone else I had pictured a freckly Irish colleen with yards of coppery curls – an actress, perhaps, or a Gaelic poet. I didn't know whether I felt angrier with him or with Agatha for their duplicity.

A lot of things were falling into place now. Like the fact that Greg seemed to know much more about me than I had ever told him (I had believed this to be a kind of natural empathy between us). And Agatha, who apparently had plans for me as a scriptwriter but had never seen my show.

'Don't fuck your clients!' she had said. 'It causes untold problems.'

Well, it would, wouldn't it, especially if the client in question was half your age. The image of them writhing about together in her bath made me want to retch. Her wrinkly arms, the skin not quite taut, gripping his perfect smooth, creamy back, his glossy curls flopping against her mottled veiny thighs. Her face, alert and greedy for him, peered over his shoulder in my imagination and laughed at me.

How could he do that when he had had blissful sex with me only hours before? The tape must have been recorded on the Thursday or Friday, and I had seen Greg on the Wednesday night. Had she known? Had he told her? Was that why she had called me drunk on Saturday? Was he the person who had sent the single red rose to the crematorium?

Why did it always happen to me? Why couldn't I, for once in my life, meet a nice man, with no complications, instead of ending up in sordid love triangles? I stamped round my flat, feeling as angry and frustrated as a child. I threw myself on the sofa and screamed into the cushions, my feet kicking wildly, my fists pounding the rough linen material until they hurt. I felt impotent and utterly alone. There was no one I could talk to. My mother would try to calm me down with well-intentioned platitudes, Martin wouldn't be able to resist saying that he had told me so, the rest of my friends would think I had gone crazy, and Stephanie, well, Stephanie would probably say that all this rage was a good thing and give me the number of a primal-scream therapist.

My anger subsided as suddenly as it had arrived, just like the end of the tantrums I could vaguely remember from when I was five years old. I began to feel utterly alone and desolate. I had no real options. I had given up my career, couldn't hope to make a living from acting and had been dismissed as a temporary secretary. Why had I got myself into this situation?

And why did I always choose impossible men? Maybe Stephanie's psychological explanations weren't so far out. Maybe I was always searching for some replacement for my father. Maybe this was something I had to deal with before I could really get on with my life. Perhaps I couldn't have a proper relationship with a man until I had resolved the relationship with him. After all, he had abandoned me and that must have affected me deeply.

I didn't think I had ever minded so much the physical absence, but I remembered the terrible empty, bitter feeling I had had when I realized, I suppose when I was about ten, that he wasn't going to write to me any more. I have very little memory of the year after he stopped writing except running downstairs every morning looking for the post. My mother must have realized sooner than

I did that the correspondence had ended, because she always tried to make breakfast special, distracting me with games and indulging me with food. I was envied at school because I was allowed to choose my individual box of cereal every day from a Kellogg's Variety Pack, whereas my classmates had Corn Flakes out of a big box. I always received my own postcard from any friend of Mum who happened to be on holiday. But it wasn't the same as those brief little notes scribbled on the back of drawings or watercolours that my father used to send. A year after the date of the last one, I burnt them all.

I sat on my sofa feeling numb. I tried to think positive thoughts. When I was at the bank I felt trapped in the rat race. At the time I had been sure that anything would be better. Well, now at least I was free. Extremely free. Rather more free than I would honestly have liked. If I were sensible I should grasp the opportunity of my freedom and go to live aboad for a while, I thought. I could try to meet the errant Marcus Fitt and talk to him and perhaps that would help. Perhaps now that I was an adult it was my responsibility too. It was no good dwelling on how badly I had been treated. Maybe I should go and confront him. Turn up on his doorstep and tell him what a bastard he had been. I thought about those awful programmes on television where long-lost relatives are reunited. Our meeting would not be all tears and hugs and sentiment. I imagined him opening the door and me throwing a bucket of water over him, and I couldn't stop myself giggling.

And since I was thinking about giving men a piece of my mind, I picked up the phone.

Disconcertingly, Greg sounded delighted to hear from me, even though I had woken him up. It was after two o'clock in the afternoon, but he was working in the evenings, he explained.

'Sophie! I'm so glad you called! I've been wanting to speak to you so much, but I haven't dared ring.'

'Why?' I was sounding as frosty as I could.

'Well, I wanted to check how you were. I've been feeling terrible about poor old Agatha. And I knew you would be too. I know you liked her ... Well, we both did.'

Yes, but not in quite the same way, I thought.

'Also, you know,' he went on tentatively, 'I've been thinking a lot about you. I was kind of hoping that you might have relaxed your rules.'

His other lover was hardly cold and yet he was flirting with me as if nothing had happened.

'Well,' I said, 'there are a couple of things I wouldn't mind discussing —'

'Great!' he interrupted. 'When can we meet?'

'Tonight?'

'Oh. Tonight's a bit difficult. We're doing a night location scene in Kilburn. But tomorrow —'

'I'm going away tomorrow,' I lied. I didn't want this thing to drag on any longer.

'Well, look, why don't you come up to Kilburn. It's not too far from you, is it? There's a hell of a lot of hanging around between shots. We could have a drink together.'

'Fine.' He gave me the address of the pub they were filming in and said that he was looking forward to it already.

The bank manager at Barclays Regent Street branch was as helpful as he could be in the circumstances. He said that he remembered the conversation with Miss

Brown. Indeed, he added ruefully, conversations with Miss Brown were generally very memorable. I told him that she was dead and he awkwardly offered his condolences. I explained who I was and showed him the letter. But he shook his head and said that he couldn't accept it. With the greatest respect, he said (why do people always use that phrase when they mean completely the opposite?), the letter was unsigned and there was no way he could verify it. I thought about telling him I had kept the tape, but felt it might be unwise. In any case it was a matter for the executors, he said, and he would await their instructions. Which is how I came to ring Dorothy again. I had completely forgotten leaving the earlier message.

'Sophie!' she said, before I had had a chance to explain why I was calling. 'I'm so very glad you've rung! I have been trying to ring you back, but that awful woman always answers the phone.'

She was speaking as if we were long-lost friends. I tried to contain my surprise.

'Look,' she continued, 'are you free for lunch tomorrow?'

I said that I was.

'Well, let me buy you lunch somewhere. How about Kettner's. No, maybe that's a little near . . . You suggest somewhere.'

There was a new and incredibly expensive Italian restaurant a few streets away from where I live. If Dorothy were paying, I thought, why not?

'Marvellous idea. I've read the reviews,' she said. 'I'll book it for one o'clock. Or would one-fifteen be more convenient? Now, one further favour . . . Would you mind keeping our meeting confidential for the moment?'

I said that I would be happy to. She was apparently

unaware that I had been fired. When she rang off I realized that I was still holding Agatha's letter to the bank manager in my hand and I hadn't had a chance to mention it.

It had just begun to get dark, but there were hours to kill before my appointment with Greg. In my new mood of optimism I decided that I deserved a little pampering. Given that I had only hours before I lost any means of supporting myself, it was reckless of me to spend the rest of the day in the Sanctuary, but it was exactly what I needed, and heavens, I thought, my credit-card bills were so large anyway, what difference would another £100 make?

It had stopped raining by the time I left. I had swum, had a rub-down with sea salt and finally been plonked in a very deep, steaming herbal bath, where I had fallen fast asleep. The chill November air acted like the final phase of a sauna and I had a delicious clean feeling all over. On consideration, it was quite a relief to have been fired. After tomorrow I needn't think any more about the gruesome events of the last weeks. Tonight would wrap up the untidy details of my relationship with Greg, tomorrow I would be able to tell Dorothy exactly what I thought of her and her bloody sister. Then, I decided, I might just take Reg up on his offer of a winter-break holiday. To blow away the cobwebs, as he would say.

24

Although I hadn't been there before, it was easy to find
the pub where we were to meet because the street had
been cordoned off and was lit up with arc lamps. There
were several lorries filled with equipment, and an enormous catering van from which arose a great cloud of
frying-bacon-scented steam. I stood a little way away
and watched them film the scene. As far as I could see,
because there were lots of people milling around between
me and the cameras, they were filming Greg and a
couple of other young men approaching the pub. There
didn't appear to be any dialogue, but the director was
unhappy with the way they were walking and kept on
making them do it again. After about an hour I was
frozen and dying for one of the doorstep sandwiches
everyone else was eating. It was approaching eleven
o'clock and the other pubs in the area were closing. I
realized that if they didn't finish soon Greg and I
wouldn't have a chance to go for a drink.

The director finally shouted, 'OK, we'll print that
one', and the crew started packing up. The pub
switched off its lights and the actors, who had been
doing nothing but make a pub-like noise inside, put on
coats and started walking off in the direction of the
tube.

I noticed Greg talking to the director. He looked very
serious. Then the director patted him on the shoulder
and they parted. Greg began to look around, as if

remembering that he was meant to be meeting me there, so I walked towards him.

'Hi! How long have you been here?'

'About an hour.'

'Mmm, you look cold.' He bent forward to kiss me. I took a step back. His kiss fell on air and he straightened up. It was all very awkward.

'So where shall we go?' he said.

'Well, everything's closed now,' I said, a bit petulantly.

'Let's get this taxi,' he said, hailing it, and before I could protest he had bundled me in and switched on the heater.

'That's better. Now, your place or mine?'

'Mine,' I stammered. I couldn't believe that he just expected to come back with me. I planned to get out when we got there and let him take the taxi on.

'What did you think?' he asked.

'About what?'

'The film.'

'All I saw were three people walking down the street. It seemed a huge operation for something so simple. Couldn't you have shot that in a studio?'

'It wouldn't look the same,' he said.

'Well, I'm delighted my licence fees are being so well spent.' It was a ridiculously pompous thing to say. I started to laugh.

'What?' he asked, looking at me with his gloriously innocent expression.

'Actually, I've never bothered to get a television licence,' I confessed. 'I always panic terribly when those adverts come on TV. I've even got a pair of wire cutters by the socket.'

'Why?'

'Oh, someone once told me that if your television isn't connected then you can't be fined. My plan is to cut the plug off before the inspectors get into the flat.'

He started laughing now.

'Crazy lady,' he said, and put his arm round me.

I wished that he wasn't so handsome. I was finding it impossible to look at him and say what I wanted to say. When we arrived at my place he was out of the taxi before I could protest.

The only thing I had in the flat to drink was a bottle of champagne. I offered him it, half hoping he would refuse. It was rather a good bottle that I had bought in Duty Free on my last business trip to New York. I had intended to drink it with Jerry to toast our breaking up. As it turned out, our separation was rather more perfunctory and I hadn't had the heart to open it since. I had found myself having worryingly sentimental feelings about Jerry recently. He was a bastard, but at least he didn't pretend to be anything else. I had known where I was with him, even though it wasn't a great place to be. Greg, on the other hand, looked like, and did a brilliant impression of, an angel. That made him more dangerous. He popped the cork and poured the liquid that hadn't frothed on to the floor into the two glasses I was holding.

'Can I propose a toast?' he asked.

I held my glass in the air without much enthusiasm.

'To Agatha. I think she would have approved, don't you?'

This was too much for me.

'You fucking bastard,' I said quietly. I lowered my glass, went into the kitchen and poured the $10 worth of golden foaming liquid into the sink. He followed me.

'And now I think you'd better go,' I said without turning round.

'Oh no. Not again, Sophie. You can't keep inviting me back here and then asking me to leave. It's not fair.' His voice was light and jokey.

'*Not fair!*' I screamed. 'You've got a fucking nerve. haven't you? Do you think what you did to me, and to Agatha for that matter, was fair?'

'What are you talking about?' he said in a quiet, calm voice.

'God, you're even more of a shit than I thought. *I know, Greg, I know what was going on!*'

'Whoa. Steady on, Sophie. You've got to calm down now and talk to me.'

'I don't want to talk to you,' I shouted. 'Just get out. *Get out!*'

'Listen, darling –'

'*Don't call me darling!*'

'Listen. I made a mistake, last time. I shouldn't have said what I said. This time I'm not going. So stop shouting and sit down and talk to me.'

'I won't.' And to show him that I meant it, I marched out of the room, into the bathroom and locked the door.

I expected to hear the door bang, or at least click, as he left, but there wasn't a sound. After a while there was. It was the Beatles song 'Here, There and Everywhere'. He was obviously making himself comfortable in my living room listening to my CDs. I resolved to spend the night, or however long it took, in the bathroom. He must get bored some time and leave. I put the cover down and sat on the toilet. It was like being held hostage in my own house. Why was he playing this game? I couldn't understand it. Unless . . . Unless he had a better reason for denying that he and Agatha had been intimate. Greg had seen Agatha before she died. I remembered my plan, lying under his very nose in my living room, with her last days mapped out and his name blazoned across it in red, like blood.

I had been so preoccupied since hearing the tape by the fact that Greg and Agatha had been having an affair that I hadn't stopped to consider the other implications of his presence in her flat. As far as I knew, he was the only person after Dorothy to see her conscious. So what had happened? Had he perhaps begun to regret his affair and thought of a way of getting rid of her? It would have been easy enough to slip an overdose into the post-coital drinks I imagined they had shared. But why? Surely not because he had started to like me and seen the impossibility of carrying on a relationship with both of us simultaneously. No. I may be attractive, but I'm hardly *femme-fatale* material. Maybe she had found out about us and threatened to ruin his career? I didn't think that was likely. He was already being talked about as one of the future faces of the 1990s. He had been interviewed for *Esquire's* New Year edition. He didn't need Agatha's goodwill that much. There simply wasn't a logical motive, but I couldn't dismiss the circumstantial evidence that he had been there.

I began to feel rather frightened. I was hardly safe in my bathroom with its slender bolt if there were indeed a murderer drinking champagne and listening to *Revolver* in my living room. My mind was racing. I remembered the note that Mr Middlemarch had shown me. It said 'SOPHIE LIST'. Perhaps Agatha was trying to say 'Sophie Listen'! Perhaps her pen had run out. Had she been pointing me towards the tape-recorder, where she knew I would hear her meeting Greg? But that was ridiculous, because she had left the tape on inadvertently. She had obviously been unaware that she was recording herself.

'Come out, come out, or I'll blow your door down!' he said, laughing from behind the door.

'Go away!' It seemed an entirely inadequate response. My heart started beating in my head and my pulse rate had gone up.

'Listen, you crazy woman,' he said, 'come out and talk to me.'

'Why?' I wished there were a window I could climb out of, but my bathroom is entirely enclosed, with only a Vent-axia for ventilation, which made it difficult to hear him when he spoke quietly. I moved closer to the door.

'Because I want to talk to you. You're making me nervous. I thought I was falling for an eccentric, but this is getting silly.'

'What do you mean, falling for?'

'I mean I like you, Sophie, I like you a lot, you know. Look, we can't have a conversation like this on either side of a door. I'm not very good at this, but I'm trying. I know it may not mean anything to you, but I want to tell you something, but I can't tell a door, you know . . .'

His voice was getting quieter and quieter. I switched the Vent-axia off and considered my options. If I thought about it calmly, Greg was not a violent man. I had never felt remotely physically threatened in his presence. In fact, I had always felt, even tonight, enveloped in respect and warmth. There had been witnesses to our meeting earlier on. So, if anything happened to me . . . I didn't want to think about that. Perhaps, if I played a cool hand, I could get him out of the flat without endangering myself. He was obviously not going to go until I came out, and he could survive longer than me. He had my flat at his disposal; I had only a supply of water and the claustrophobia of my bathroom, with its mottled beige tiles and avocado suite which I had always loathed and meant to change. I wished now that I had, because the prospect of holding out a night there appalled me.

'I'll come out on one condition,' I said, thinking as I spoke.

'What?'

'I'll come out on one condition, and that is that you wait for me outside and we go for a walk. I need some fresh air.'

'So, I have to wait downstairs? Outside the cake shop? Will that do?' He was humouring me. I detected a chuckle in his voice.

'Yup,' I said, trying not to let my voice sound too triumphant.

'I'm sure you have your reasons.'

'I do.'

'OK,' he said.

I heard him opening the door to the flat and then walking down the communal staircase. When I was sure he had reached the bottom I unlocked the bathroom door, leapt to my flat door and double-locked it, then went into the front room.

He was standing shivering in the cold outside the patisserie as we had just arranged. I noticed that he had left his lined leather biker's jacket on my sofa. He looked up at the window and waved. I sat down on the sofa rather pleased with myself, until the entryphone started to ring.

'For God's sake, give me my jacket at least,' he said, now somewhat annoyed.

Serves you right, I thought. I was going to throw it down to him, but when I picked it up change and a couple of biros fell out of the pockets. I didn't think I could come to any harm if I took it down to him rather than throwing it out of the window.

25

'One day we will laugh at this,' he said.

I didn't think I ever would, but as time has passed I have. Sometimes almost hysterically, and always with a bittersweet tinge of regret.

We were sitting in an all-night kebab bar on the Chalk Farm Road. Greg drank a glass of retsina while I munched my way through a mixed kebab which contained doner, souvlaki and those delicious little sausages flavoured with fresh flat-leaf parsley. I have become quite a connoisseur of Greek food since living in the borough of Camden.

I had been going to hand him his jacket at arm's length, then slam the door and scuttle back to the safety of my flat, but he had caught my hand and drawn me towards him and kissed me on the mouth. I had been surprised by the strength of his embrace and had succumbed to it. In the open air, the danger seemed to have dissipated.

'Mmmmm,' he said when we separated.

'Is that how it was with her?' I said meanly.

'No,' he said. 'It's never been like that with anyone else.'

I ought to have felt disgusted. In fact I felt rather pleased with myself.

'So why were you fucking her?' I said crisply.

'Well, I know it's difficult to explain, but Maeve and I had a lot of history –'

'Who's Maeve?'

'My girlfriend . . . Well, my ex −'

'Oh, come on!' I interrupted. 'I know, you know.'

'You keep saying this, Sophie, and saying it with a horrible look that doesn't suit you. What is your problem?'

'Do I have to spell it out?'

'Yes. You do.'

'I know, Greg, that you were having an affair with Agatha −' He held up his hand in protest and astonishment, but I persisted with the evidence, telling him everything that I had worked out, ending with those four unambiguous words on the tape.

Silence as he turned away and looked blankly into the patisserie window, as if trying to find inspiration from the empty cakestands. When he turned back, his eyes were watery sad.

'Do you really believe that?' he asked solemnly.

As soon as he said it I had a sinking feeling.

'Well . . .'

'You're right in one thing, no, maybe two things . . . I was there on Thursday afternoon. And I think that Agatha did, no, I know that she did, want to. Not then, but other times. She had quite a reputation, you know. You must have known that? I mean, how many women are there on her client list? She was a terrible flirt.'

'So why were you there?'

'Sophie, you know, this really isn't worthy of you. I was there because I went to visit my agent, no, my friend. She had been really good to me, you know, and I liked her. Yes, it had been more than an agent-stroke-client relationship, but before you get that look of self-satisfaction stuck on your face − take care, Sophie, that the wind doesn't change when you look like that − not that much more. We had often had a drink together, and discussed things other than work, yeah, like the fact that I had seen your act. No, she didn't know about us, if that's what you're thinking ... I thought she was a lonely person essentially. I've been lonely too here. You know that. So I went to see Agatha, because she was a friend who was ill, and when I got there she was about to have a bath and a drink and I must have said could I join her, because you heard it on the tape. If you'd have asked me to tell you what I said, I would have said I asked if I could have a drink too. But apparently, according to your evidence, as you insist on calling it, I said, could I join her. Well, I did join her. We both had a whisky – a Scotch. She was always in favour of the Scotch, not the Irish – I used to jeer her with it. Then she did go and have a bath, yeah, so I did go and sit on the side of her amazing bath. Did you ever see that bath? What a strange indulgence in that flat! And yeah, I did see her covered in bubbles in that bath. We chatted and she was on great form. She was so pleased with herself, because she had had a reconciliation with her sister. She was almost euphoric. That's why I've been so sad ever since. She really did seem so happy then.'

'And what happened?' I faltered.

'Well, nothing really. I had to go to work, so I left. No. Wait a minute, since you're after every detail ... She asked me to bring her another drink. I went to get one from the living room. The phone was ringing. She called from her bath, "Darling!" ... But she called everyone darling.'

I nodded.

'"Darling, can you pick that up?" she said. I remember because it was the first time I had ever picked up a portable phone. I picked it up and there was nothing. I shouted this back to her. "Stupid Irishman," she said, "flick the 'on' switch and pull up the aerial!" So I did. Somebody asked for her. I took the phone to her in the bath . . . After that her mood changed.'

'And what happened?'

'Well, she was speaking to your man on the phone. It didn't sound a very friendly conversation. I handed her a drink and indicated that I had to go. She just waved at me. And I let myself out.'

'And that was on Thursday?'

'Yeah. That was the last time I saw her.'

'I don't know what to say.'

We stood in silence for a couple of minutes. I wished that the patisserie were open. I felt cold and empty.

'No. Well, I think I'll be on my way.'

I couldn't bear it if he just left, like that, but I somehow knew that if I invited him in again he would refuse.

'I'm starving!' I said, realizing that I hadn't eaten all day. 'Would you mind walking me down to get a take-away? It's a bit late and I don't like the railway bridge in the dark.'

We walked down the road, over the railway bridge and into the nearest kebab bar. Greg's hands were firmly in his pockets. I tried to explain why I had thought what I had thought, but he was silent. A sense of disillusion hung around him. To someone who had once told me that his favourite characteristic was generosity, I must have seemed a very mean-minded and petty character. I tried to pick up the subject of Maeve, but he just stared blankly at me, silently admonishing me for my lack of subtlety.

'One day we will laugh at this,' he said. But he didn't smile.

26

Greg walked me back to my flat and I waited with him at the bottom of Primrose Hill for a taxi. We discussed whether it was cold enough for snow and then fell silent. I began thinking about his account of Thursday night.

'You know when you last saw Agatha?' I suddenly said.

'Look, I really don't want to discuss that any more.'

'I'm not trying to discuss it. It's just I was wondering, was Chutney there?'

He looked at me as if I had flipped.

'You know, Chutney, Agatha's cat.'

'Oh, is that what it's called! Yeah. Of course. When did you ever see her without that cat? I nearly broke my neck tripping over him when I took the phone in to Agatha. Oh, here's one!'

A taxi with its orange light indicating that it was free had just appeared at the top of the hill.

'And the phone call . . . that seemed to upset her. Was it her partner? Can you remember?'

He thought for a moment. 'No, I don't think so. More of an accent. I try not to overhear other people's conversations.'

'Ouch,' I said, 'point taken. But you don't think it was him?'

The taxi had pulled up alongside us. Greg opened the door and clambered in.

'I can't remember. What on earth does it matter? Bye, Sophie . . . Wait a minute,' he said as he closed the door. 'It couldn't have been her partner on the phone, because he was just coming up the drive when I left.'

'Anthony White? Are you sure?'

'Of course I'm sure − You can't mistake that stupid car. Anyway, he waved at me . . .'

I tried to keep the image of Greg looking out of the taxi window in my mind for as long as I could. His face was so unusually beautiful that I found it difficult to recall in his absence. It always slightly unbalanced me when I saw him again. This time I wouldn't be seeing him again, except perhaps on television. I felt empty and sad and yet I don't think I ever really believed that Greg and I would have a proper relationship. He was so perfect, it was like fucking a film star in the role you liked best (for me it's a difficult choice between Laurence Harvey in *Room at the Top* and Paul Newman in *Sweet Bird of Youth*).

I couldn't sleep, even though I felt totally exhausted. The more I thought about it, the more sure I was that there was something amiss about Agatha's death. If this had been a mystery novel, so far I wouldn't have made a very good detective. My first suspect, Mr Weirdo Watt, had been a very long shot, and I had managed to lose a lover and potential friend by suspecting Greg. I didn't want to make another wrong move, but it did seem odd to me that Anthony White, who had everything to gain from it, had at first not seemed surprised by Agatha's death. Then he had changed his theory about it, then on the day when I was going to confront him about this (I now remembered dimly from the morning, it seemed so long ago), he had sacked me. Also he was now the last person, as far as I knew, to have seen her conscious. He had looked very awkward, I recalled, when I had asked him when he last spoke to her, and had implied that they had talked only on the phone.

I wondered whether I should ring Mr Middlemarch in the morning, but then remembered that I was having lunch with Dorothy − another suspect, after all − so I decided to wait until after that, in case I found out anything more.

It was three in the morning but I still couldn't sleep. I got up, put on my white towelling robe, went into my living room and curled up on the sofa with the second half of *The Hairs in the Sink*.

At the beginning of the second act, Johnny realizes that there is something peculiar about the weird three-some he is sharing a house with. He tries first of all to become matey with Sid, but comes up against a brick wall of loyalty, then Johnny and Jemima start having a very loud and passionate sexual relationship. Bella is eaten up by jealousy, as, to an extent, is Sid. Sid tells Bella that he doesn't think that Johnny loves Jemima, he just wants to find out their secret. Seeing a way to ensnare Johnny herself, Bella tells him the secret. In the play, the secret is that Jemima, Bella and Sid are merely squatting in the house. The owners are away on holiday. They have broken in and have no right to be there at all. Johnny immediately sees that he must move on quickly. He has always found it strange that the others stay indoors all the time, although the weather is hot. He has a job, and must have been seen coming to and going from the house. In any case, they will have to move sooner or later. He calls everyone together and tells them his plan for getting them out safely. Bella agrees to go with him. Sid hovers around, waiting for a lead. Jemima simply frowns regally as if she has no idea what he is talking about.

The ending of the play is ambiguous. Has Jemima deluded herself to the point where she is now mad and believes that she is the lady of the house, or is she pretending in order to show Johnny (and Bella) that she is immune to their betrayal? In the final scene Johnny and Bella leave in confusion. Bella tries to say goodbye, but is ignored. The last stage direction reads: 'Spotlight on Jemima's impassive face. Sound of keys in the lock as the owners of the house return.'

27

'I'm sure you've been wondering why I've asked you here,' said Dorothy.

That was something of an understatement. I gave a kind of nod.

'Well, the whole thing, as I'm sure you can imagine, has rather upset me. I know that I've been a bit off-hand and I wanted to offer a kind of olive branch . . .' She was quite distressingly like Agatha in both appearance and manner. Right down to the peculiar aristocratic way of belittling emotions.

I mumbled something about there being no need, as the waiter hovered around for our order. Dorothy chose half a dozen oysters to start. I looked for something that would be easy to eat and settled on a salad of rocket, sun-dried tomatoes and shaved Parmesan. It sounded less interesting than the squid-ink spaghetti with langoustine salsa, but I was wearing a cream polo-neck sweater, which was almost a guarantee of spillage. It was one of those new Italian restaurants that serves food bearing no relation to anything you've ever eaten in Italy. The menu is all roasted peppers, porcini and grilled polenta; everything is drizzled with olive oil so extra extra virgin that you wonder why they don't just leave a bowl of olives on the table rather than going to all the trouble of pressing them. We both chose the pan-seared calves' liver with a raspberry and balsamic vinegar salsa. (Why is it that a few years ago you couldn't eat anything that wasn't surrounded by a coulis of some fruit or other and now you can't have food that isn't smothered in salsa, whatever that may be?) The waiter was dressed entirely in black and looked as likely to produce a smile as a great phallic grinder from behind his back and shout in a ludicrous Italian accent 'Some pepper?' as Italian waiters used to. What with the minimal décor and the unseasonal air-conditioning, it was like eating in a very trendy morgue.

'You see,' she continued, 'I'm going to try, but I'm not sure I'll cope ... I have to say, I do need some help. I know it's a lot to ask, but do you think you might ...?'

I let her question hang in the air, hoping that she would carry on and give me a clue as to what she was talking about. She didn't, so I had to ask.

'What do you mean?'

'Has no one told you?'

'What?'

'Well, I suppose it's understandable, given Tony's present frame of mind ... You see, I have inherited everything. All Agatha's shares. Everything. I'm the next of kin, and she died without a will – What's the word for that, I should know ... intestate – She always was so bad about paperwork.'

'Oh ...' My first thought was relief that I had been a little more circumspect this time about ringing Mr Middlemarch, since my third suspect's main motive had just disappeared.

'I had assumed Anthony had inherited,' I said.

He had been behaving as if he had an automatic right to carry on representing Agatha's clients. I wasn't sure how one could exactly bequeath an agency, since the livelihood depended so much on the loyalty of the clients, but I assumed, since he had spent so much time at the lawyers recently, that the company was now his.

'Well, of course, it must have been a terrible blow for him, because they were close. First she kills herself, without leaving him a note or anything, and then he gets nothing.' I thought I almost detected glee in her voice.

'But I thought Anthony thought that it might be an accident.'

'Well, of course, that's what he's trying to say now. It's desperate really. He doesn't really believe that, but he's got to leave open the possibility of doubt, because there is a life insurance policy. He organized that for both of them because it was a tax-deductible expense on the company. He is the sole beneficiary of that, but there's a clause that says it's nullified by suicide. When he found that out he started to say that he thought it might have been an accident. He even told Mr Middlemarch that he thought you would support him. Mr Middlemarch realized the problem. He says that coroners are usually very understanding about these things.'

I noticed, as she picked up her first oyster, that her hand was shaking uncontrollably.

'I say,' she said, 'it's awfully depressing talking about it, isn't it? Shall we have some wine?'

Before I had a chance to respond, she waved down a passing waiter and ordered a bottle of Chianti. She drank two glasses in quick succession and a pink glow suffused her face. Although she was wearing a good deal of foundation and face powder, little purple veins began to show through the camouflage on her nose.

'What I'm not sure of,' I ventured, 'is how I can help?'

'By doing exactly what you are.'

'Which is?'

'Keeping the whole thing going. You know, just till I find my feet. I mean, she would have wanted me to continue . . . don't you think? I've given it a great deal of thought. I haven't even really told Jack yet. I can't until I've got it all organized. Tony's been trying to dissuade me, of course. I suppose it's partly that I want to show him that I can. I haven't had a job for years, but . . . He's trying to buy me out. It's all very well, but if he hadn't been so horrible to me, just helping Agatha drive me out . . . I haven't forgotten that, you know . . . I know I'm not really entitled to all of it, but he'd be the first to do me out of anything if he had half a chance . . . Anyway, you see, I'm a bit rusty about the business and I will need a little help. Agatha told me you were very bright —'

'But I was fired by Anthony, yesterday, or perhaps fired isn't the word. What do Americans say? Let go. It always sounds so much more humane. I was let go . . .'

She looked at me in surprise. Then poured herself another glass. Five oysters remained untouched on her plate.

'Typical. The bastard. He always was one step ahead of me,' she said, suddenly dropping the polite façade as what I had just said dawned on her. 'I suppose he thinks I won't be able to do it without your help. But he's forgotten,' she continued, regaining her composure, 'I'm in charge now and I am re-employing you.'

'However,' I said curtly, 'I am not absolutely sure that I want the job.'

For a second, she looked very cross.

'Agatha said you were sharp,' she said. 'I will, of course, offer you more money.'

'I'm still not sure,' I countered, holding her eyes. She

seemed to have all the arrogance of her sister, but none of the charm.

Our standoff was interrupted by the waiter inquiring whether we had finished our first course. Dorothy said we had and ordered another bottle.

'There's one thing that puzzles me,' I said tentatively. 'Forgive me for inquiring, but my information was that you and Agatha were estranged. I was under the impression that you hadn't spoken to each other for years, until last Wednesday.'

'But we hadn't ... That is, of course, what is so appalling for me now. I keep thinking that if only I hadn't gone to her, then none of this would have happened. I blame myself. I blame myself. I know it's stupid but I do, you see ...' The carefully groomed composure was slipping. She fell silent and drank another glass of wine. I had hardly touched mine.

'Gone to her?' I repeated.

'You see, I wouldn't have. Or rather, I shouldn't have ... It all seems so trivial now. You know how easily these things can get out of proportion in families?' She looked at me for support. 'Or perhaps you don't. I imagine that you have a nice ordinary family ...'

I just nodded.

'Well, of course, ours, if you can call it a family, was positively Tolstoyan in its unhappiness. Well, if not Tolstoyan, certainly Chekovian ... Yes, that's more like it. Agatha would have approved of that,' she mused, smiling to herself. 'What if there had been two sisters, not three? We used to play this game together, you know –'

'The What if? game?'

'Yes. Did she tell you about that? She did say to me that she had found a soulmate in her temp. That's why I thought ... I thought I could trust you, you see.' Her speech was becoming more and more slurred. I almost felt I was taking advantage of her drunkenness by encouraging her to continue.

'So you went to her . . .'

'Well, you see, last week . . . No, it wasn't last week, was it? . . . Last week was the lawyers, and the funeral, that's what happened last week . . .' She seemed almost to be talking to herself now. 'Whenever it was, anyway, the week before last . . . I suppose I went under false pretences, really. One of our friends who is a client of hers − such a small world, the theatre − had mentioned that she was off work, sick − unheard of, for Agatha, of course − so I made it an excuse to ring her. I asked her if I could help. Of course, you know she is absolutely hopeless at looking after herself. Her idea of a meal is a Marmite sandwich. And did you see the kitchen? It took me an hour of solid cleaning to get it into a fit state for cooking. There was so much rubbish I couldn't even lift the bag out of the bin. We hadn't spoken to one another properly for years and years. I always used to try at Christmas, and I sent photographs. That sort of thing. When Bob got married she sent him a £1,000 as a wedding present, but Jack made him send it back . . . She was surprised to hear from me but she didn't resist, as she had done before. She said it was probably about time we behaved like adults. So I offered to cook her dinner . . . Of course, I had an ulterior motive . . .'

At this point the waiter annoyingly arrived with the second course, said 'Enjoy your meal' in a robotic monotone, then disappeared. I hoped that Dorothy had not been too distracted. I downed my almost full glass of wine in the hope that it would encourage her to continue. She obliged by starting on the next bottle.

'You see, Jack was having so much difficulty even

getting his work read ... I thought that maybe she could put in a word. I didn't expect her to represent him. He wouldn't accept that even if she had offered, but I thought if she could just discreetly help, for my sake, really. Life was becoming intolerable. Of course, I arrived at her flat determined to ask her in an unemotional way, but we had a few cocktails ... I'm not used to whisky, you see, and it just tastes like lemonade the way Agatha makes it, and I ended up telling her everything. I'm not very good at keeping secrets, you see ...'

I felt that I had now become almost superfluous to the monologue. Perhaps she hadn't been allowed to talk out her feelings at home. I knew that it was important for her to talk. Stephanie had told me all about the seven stages of grief, and I knew that one of them was talking, although I couldn't remember the others. So I listened.

I started to slice the liver on my plate; it ran with watery pink blood once it had been cut. I thought about Agatha's liver, isolated on a pathologist's table, and wondered if it had looked like this. I put down my knife and fork.

I tried to piece the story together. Dorothy had gone to ask Agatha to help because Jack was becoming impossible to live with because nobody would read his work. I remembered Agatha's utter contempt for his work and thought how pointless Dorothy's begging mission had been.

'... I feel so disloyal now. But Agatha had a way of getting things out of me and when I told her, she persuaded me that I must leave him ... I knew what she was saying was right. It always seems right when I talk about it with other people, but I can never bring myself to. And then he gets better, as if he knows ... And I don't know whether I am just being silly or not. It's not so simple –'

'But Agatha thought it was?'

'Yes. She seemed almost happy about it. For a few hours it was just like before. We were plotting it all together. She said she would help me. She said that I would be all right. She said it would be just like before, you see –'

'Just like before Jack took you away?' I was guessing but, having finished his play in the early hours of the morning, I felt I knew the story.

'Yes. Just like that.' For a moment, even with her grey hair and make-up, Dorothy looked like a little girl. Then her face crumpled and she began to cry.

28

In the end I regretted having chosen the restaurant, because I had to pay the extortionate bill for a couple of bottles of average house wine. We had eaten about four ounces of food between us, but she was in such a state I had to get her out of there.

I learned a lot more about the Brown sisters that afternoon as Dorothy, between bouts of grief and with gentle prodding, rambled on and on, sitting, sometimes lying, on my sofa.

They had been orphaned in the war and were fostered out to a woman they called 'Mum'. This must have been the old lady at the funeral. They had spent the war years roller-skating in the blitzed streets of London and, when the sirens sounded, entertaining their neighbours in bomb shelters with plays. Amy, who thought her name altogether too silly and insisted on being called Agatha, was always the leader. Her sister, younger by only eighteen months, looked on adoringly. When they had saved tuppence of their pocket money, they would go to the Boot's library and borrow books.

The more she read, the more Agatha dreamt of being born into a different class, and when they were adolescents, they ran away and pretended, which was easier than one might have imagined at that time, when so many people were rootless because of the war, to have come from somewhere else. Agatha plotted out their background and Dorothy joined in the game. Agatha was always having to test Dorothy, because she was inclined to give them away, but she learned and, by the time they reached their twenties, they had consolidated their position in the bohemian society of the late 1950s. Agatha, always the entrepreneur, had set herself up as an agent. Dorothy, as far as I could tell, was nothing more than her assistant, but they called the agency Brown and Brown none the less. And then Tony White had appeared. He had read about the two charming, successful Brown sisters in a gossip column.

He was another street kid, a younger one, who had always wanted to be in their plays, but had been excluded by Agatha. He knew all about them, so, at last, they had to let him join in. I felt that Dorothy shouldn't have been telling me all this, although why it mattered now, I couldn't decide. Maybe I had been caught up in the game myself and didn't want to know that it was all a fiction.

I now understood Jack Burton's play almost more than I wanted to. I vaguely remembered Agatha saying that it had dated terribly. She was right, of course, in that class isn't the issue it was in the 1960s any more. Or so we like to think. And it was a play about class, since you could see without knowing the background of the characters in real life, that the big house and all the beautiful things in it stood as a metaphor for the middle class, and there were tiny giveaway phrases in Bella's vocabulary, as well as obviously in Sid's. In a wider sense, though, it was a morality tale about pretending to be what you are not. With its strange Gothic setting, I felt it had a more universal appeal than some of its truly kitchen-sink contemporaries and I was surprised that it wasn't better known. The writing was always economical and witty, sometimes verging on farce, and even reading it, rather than seeing it on the stage, I had laughed in several places, and yet felt a genuine shiver of horror as the plot unravelled.

There had been all those requests in the file for the play, but none of them seemed to have resulted in contracts. None of them, now that I came to think about it, appeared to have resulted in replies.

I tried to envisage the files I had been looking at in the basement the day before. Until a photocopier was installed some time in the late 1970s, Brown and Brown secretaries had made carbon copies of correspondence on blue flimsy paper. I knew because I had waded through piles of it looking for the relevant sheet in Cormac O'Hara's file. But I was suddenly sure there hadn't been any in Jack Burton's files from 1962 and 1963.

When Dorothy started sobering up I made her a cup of tea and she sat sipping it, looking worried, trying to remember, when she heard what the time was, what she must have said in all those hours. I began to question her gently.

'When was it, exactly, that you and Agatha fell out?'

'Oh, didn't you know? It was the first night of Jack's play. Agatha was furious with him because he had changed the play in the later rehearsals and he hadn't told her –'

'What?'

'Oh, I could never understand why she made such a fuss. You see, the first version had all the characters staying in the house and he changed it so Johnny went off with Bella.'

I looked at her in disbelief. Surely she must have realized? But perhaps not. Sometimes people are so close to something they cannot see.

'So what happened?' I asked, intrigued.

'Well, they had this row and Jack got very drunk and announced at the party that he and I were getting married. It was news to me too, actually. I was overjoyed. Agatha just left. She wouldn't let me in when I got home. She was so very jealous, you see. I think she thought I had betrayed her. Well, and Jack, of course. Because they had been lovers, you know, before he and I were. But I was the one he loved, you see, and . . . I was . . . and I was pregnant.'

'Oh, I didn't know you had children.'

'Oh yes. Two boys. After college Bob got married and went to live in Australia. Then Joe followed. We miss them so much. But they're doing very well out there. Everything was fine when they were growing up. Just normal, you know. It was only when they left home, you know . . . Well, Jack decided to take early retirement from school and go back to writing . . . and it is difficult these days, more difficult, I think, than when we were young. He's been so disappointed, you know . . . and it's brought back all the disappointment from before . . . when *Hairs* bombed and then Agatha was impossible. She made it very difficult for Jack. Bad-mouthing him round London. She felt she had created him, you see, because his first two plays were unproduce-able, but she had seen his talent and nurtured it – you know how intuitive she is. I'm sure he couldn't have done it without her and I suppose she thought she could destroy him too. That night when she left the party she said to us, "Neither of you two will be any-thing without me", and, you know, in a funny kind of way, she was right. Agatha is usually right. But I thought she seemed to have mellowed with age, maybe because she was ill –'

'Wait a minute, you mean the other day?' I asked.

Dorothy was still a little incoherent from the drink. She nodded.

'She said I could come and live there to begin with, then we would get a house. Just like we planned when we were little. But I had to keep it all a secret. I'm not very good at keeping secrets, though, and when I woke up the next morning, it all seemed a bit daft to me. I mean, I hadn't her for decades and now I was meant to move in with her again. I was meant to go back . . . but I didn't.'

'To Agatha's? Did you speak to her again?'

'Well, that's why I feel so awful. I just didn't dare tell her I'd changed my mind. And Jack was being so nice. He totally understood, and he said that he would change. First he was very angry when he heard I'd been there, but he just went out on a binge on Friday night, and since then he really has been better. We've only had a couple of cross words over Chutney, but that was to be expected. I shouldn't have forgotten the letter, of course –'

'What?'

'Oh, you know, she hadn't bothered to tell us that someone wanted to produce his play. She showed me this letter from a university in America saying it was a seminal work! We had a good laugh about that. I was meant to take the letter home, but I suppose I was a bit the worse for wear and I forgot . . . I tried to find the letter afterwards, but it had gone.'

'Well, don't worry, they've written again. It was one of the things that I rang you about. It will be on Agatha's desk in the office. The other thing was,' I added, 'this letter.'

I showed her the bank manager's letter, which precipitated another burst of tears.

'That's my account number. She really did think I would leave, then.'

When she calmed down she said, 'You're being so kind. You will come and work for me, won't you?'

She looked so pathetic that I almost weakened. I felt sorry for Dorothy. She had spent her life in the shadow of her big sister and was, in so many ways, a pale imitation of her. Not nearly as confident, not as stylish, and really rather stupid. She had been beautiful, but years of cruelty (mental or physical, I didn't know, and didn't feel I could ask) and alcohol had aged her badly. Even her hair, which was cut in the same kind of bob as Agatha's had been, was a dull grey, rather than the gleaming white of her sister. But I didn't really warm to her. Even after all I had heard, there was something about Agatha that I admired. She had been a monster, but so consummately skilled a monster you almost had to take your hat off to her. It was the difference between seeing a first-rate performer and the understudy.

I told Dorothy that I had other plans. I was going to go abroad for a while. I felt that I knew too much already about the Brown sisters. I wanted to disentangle myself from their web. It seemed to me that they were both not just eccentric but rather dangerously mad. They had played the What If? game for real. And both of them had lost. There was something so self-destructive about them, it felt almost contagious.

We sat in silence for a while. Then Dorothy asked if she could use the bathroom. When she came back, freshly painted and perfumed and obviously ready to leave, I knew it would be my last chance to ask.

'Do you really believe that your sister committed suicide?'

'Oh yes . . . She was worried about her health. Not her

cold, of course, her liver. Her naturopath, or nutritionist, or whatever he's called these days, had told her to stop drinking, and then he said she should have some tests. He told the Coroner that he suspected serious liver damage, and that fits in with the post-mortem ... Well, I could see she was terrified. I'm sure that's why she agreed to see me in the first place. I think she thought she was a goner and –'

'But she seemed to be getting better when I saw her, and a friend of mine saw her later that week and said she was fine.'

'Yes, but she was brilliant at putting on an act, you know, for the outside world. Tony popped round to see her on his way home on Thursday and she wouldn't even let him in. I just don't think she could face telling him that she had seen me ... He feels terrible now because he should have tried harder, but it was his night with his son –'

'And you're sure it couldn't have been an accident?'

'Oh no. You see, Agatha hated drugs and hospitals and everything like that. She was very ill during the war, you know, and spent a lot of time in an isolation ward. And there were thirty empty sachets in the rubbish. She would rather have died than taken that stuff for thera-peutic reasons. I hope she didn't suffer too much. I mean, you saw her, didn't you? Didn't you think that she looked peaceful?'

I didn't know what to say. I would never forget Agatha's deathly face. I had tried to convince myself that it had looked peaceful, but it hadn't. It had looked rather angry and determined.

'If only I had been brave enough to ring her ...' Dorothy's voice was beginning to waver again.

'We all feel that,' I said, trying to reassure her, as I

had tried to reassure myself countless times. 'But unless you get to someone very quickly with that kind of overdose, there's not a lot you can do, apparently.'

'No,' said Dorothy. 'I suppose not.'

I put her into a taxi at about seven o'clock.

'Are you sure you won't change your mind?' she asked.

I said I was sorry. I knew she could never hope to keep the agency going. It was totally irrational of her to think she could. Anthony and Janet would be obstructive. Who could blame them? Dorothy would drink herself into oblivion. Nobody who was 'not very good at keeping secrets', as she kept saying, would last a day in a world that deals in confidences. I didn't want to stand on deck bailing out hopelessly as the ship inevitably sank.

We both tried to end the conversation on a friendly note, Dorothy shaking my hand and wishing me all the best. I told her to give Chutney a stroke from me.

'Oh, poor Chutney,' she said wistfully. 'I'm afraid we had to have him put down. I mean, he was very old, you know, and well, Jack is so very allergic to cats . . .'

I went upstairs with a heavy heart. I rang Martin and asked if I could see him the next day. He said that he had a meeting with a client in Sussex, so he wouldn't be able to make lunch. I told him that I had lost my job and that I would explain when I next saw him. He obviously sensed the misery in my voice.

'Well, if you're off work, why don't you come down to Brighton for the day?' he suggested. 'My meeting will be over after lunch. I'm not expected back in the office. We could have an afternoon by the sea.'

The prospect of getting out of London, even for a few hours, delighted me. We agreed to meet in the lounge of the Grand Hotel.

29

I love seaside towns, especially in winter. There's something about decaying grandeur standing solidly adjacent to the flimsy trappings of an impoverished nation — candy-floss spinners, stalls piled high with Kiss-Me-Quick plastic bowler hats and Union Jack flags, My-Parents-Went-to-Brighton-and-All-I-Got-Was-This-Lousy-T-shirts flapping about on coat hangers in the icy wind — that sums up England, and all the contradictions of a post-imperial country that has lost its way.

I feel comfortably anonymous among the human debris that washes up in such places. Hell's Angels roaring down the sea front; parents huddled behind windbreaks while their hardy children, impervious to the cold, run around with fluorescent pink and yellow buckets and spades, trying to create castles from dirty pebbles; and when night comes, prostitutes whispering in the insalubrious narrow streets where the cheapest bed and breakfasts abound. It's ironic that the only time of year such towns thrive is when the political parties and the great entourage of press condescend to visit and there discuss how to improve the country's fortunes. Photo calls in fish and chip bars, fringe gatherings in flashing discos, the morning interview on the windswept beach. For a soundbite, the British public sees the seaside on its television screen and remembers what it used to be like, before it became more expensive than a package to Corfu.

'Hello, stranger!'

It was beginning to get dark when Martin interrupted my third egg-and-cress finger sandwich. I drank the dregs of my tea and suggested that we visit the pier before it closed. He put his arm round me as we walked along the promenade.

If anyone had been interested, we would have made an unlikely couple. He, in his smart suit and navy cashmere overcoat, I in old jeans, Dr Martens boots and my worn, but warm, genuine leather-sleeved baseball jacket, with 'Jerry' embroidered above my right breast and the Mets logo on the back, a treasured gift. If you could call it a gift. I had worn it home one cold morning years ago and neglected ever to give it back to him.

Martin told me about his meeting. He was reasonably optimistic that it had been a success. He asked how I had been since he last heard from me. I told him that I was enjoying the sea air so much that I didn't want to talk about it just now. He looked at me dubiously.

I don't know whether you could describe Martin as handsome. He is averagely tall, rather slight, has curly averagely brown hair, which he keeps far too short for my tastes, and nice grey eyes. He looks a bit too kind to be sexy, which is an awful thing to think, and says more about me than him, but is true, nevertheless. He is the only man I ever encountered without the slightest trace of misogyny. I looked up at him strolling dutifully along beside me, the wind whipping what there was of his hair away from his face, and thought how very much I relied on him and loved him.

We stood for a while watching the last glimmerings of real light fade away and the strings of fairy lights and pulsing neon claim their night territory. We were alone at the end of the pier, except for a couple of fishermen.

One of them reeled in a mackerel; it wriggled silver in the air for seconds before it slapped down on the wooden boards. A blob of thick fishy blood bounced up from its traumatized gills on impact and hit me just below my left eye. As I stood there, bewildered, I had a curiously strong sensation of being at a fork in my life. I could follow the signpost that said 'Go on, cry, you've had a rotten unfair time, and this just about confirms it!' or the one that said 'Oh, for heaven's sake, what's a splattering of dead fish on your face, after all!'

I began to laugh and laugh, as Martin dabbed at my cheek with his pure white cotton handkerchief, ordering me to keep still, because I was only making it worse.

The Waltzer was closed and so was the Whip. The ghost-train man was packing up. He looked at us hopefully. We walked past him and back to the newly refurbished Victorian bar we had passed on our way out to sea. Inside it was a strange mixture of plastic art deco, pink net pelmets and steam that turned to condensation on the windows and blocked out the view.

Martin raised an eyebrow when I said that I wanted an orange juice.

'I've decided to give up alcohol for a while,' I told him solemnly. Seeing what it had done to Dorothy and Agatha Brown had made me rather frightened.

He ordered a large brandy and sat down in a maroon velvet-style booth to listen to my story.

'But what I don't understand,' he said, coming back from the bar with his third brandy, and a Coke for me (I knew that I wouldn't last very long as a teetotaller, non-alcoholic drinks are so relentlessly sweet and dull), 'is why you are so convinced that it was him.'

'Well, you can't have been listening then! It's so obvious. There's this frustrated playwright, going through a mid-life crisis, and we know he has violent tendencies anyway –'

'Well, for a start, we don't know that – You said yourself that you didn't know whether Dorothy was talking about mental or physical cruelty.'

'All right, but don't keep interrupting. This is what I think happened. Dorothy, who can't keep a secret even when she is sober, goes home to Jack from Agatha's place pissed out of her head . . . She tells him where she's been. He's furious –'

'So he goes round and kills Agatha? That's ridiculous.'

'No, wait a minute. What she also tells him is that Agatha has this letter of his that's she's omitted to tell them about. She has suppressed his work.'

'What are you talking about? You said that there was one letter from an American university. That hardly amounts to all-out censorship.'

'Well, I think Jack may have put a few things together. First of all, the play had an incredibly short run considering the reviews, and how good it is. Secondly, no other agent in London will touch him, after the split. And I've seen the files. I don't think Agatha responded to any requests for the play . . . And interest is pretty short-lived in the theatre. If you leave something too long, there'll be another man of the minute. So, in effect, she killed his work.'

'Or maybe he only had one good play in him. Or maybe, since *The Hairs in the Sink* – why is it called that, by the way? – is all about Agatha, once she was out of his life, then he didn't have anything to write about,' said Martin, rather pedantically, I thought, especially since it was a valid point that did rather weaken my theory.

'Just let me continue . . . It's called that because Bella has long red hair and Jemima gets furious that she doesn't wash the sink out properly, leaving traces, you see. I think it's a metaphor for Dorothy not being able to keep a secret . . . anyway —'

'Are we back in real life now? I'm finding this a bit confusing,' Martin teased.

I glowered at him. 'We know that Agatha received a phone call that upset her the day after Dorothy's visit, from a man with an accent. She's so upset that she doesn't let Anthony in when he calls to visit. And when I go round on Sunday, the cat has been let out, and Jack is allergic to cats, so, what I think happened is that Jack insisted on going round to pick up the letter. They had a few drinks together for old times' sake. Don't forget, they had been lovers before. She's drinking hot lemon toddies, but instead of making them with lemon juice, he makes it with hot lemon drink — you know, the sort you take when you have a cold. Lots of it. He disguises the taste with honey. He's read this article that everyone seems to have read about too much paracetamol being lethal —'

'But this is pure speculation. It's just as likely, even if you believe that the phone call was from Jack, that he's ringing up to tell her that Dorothy is not coming back to her, so Agatha makes her own lethal cocktail. She's been betrayed once by Dorothy, twice is too much.'

'I've thought of that,' I said. 'But the thing is, why would she then put the empty sachets in the rubbish? And why did she let out Chutney?'

'Well, why would he put the empty sachets in the rubbish, for that matter? If he wanted it to look like suicide, then surely he would leave them there?' Martin looked triumphant, as if this were a battle of logic and his was better than mine.

'I've thought of that too ... You see, he wasn't sure whether it would work – he's hardly a contract killer, after all, and he knew that if she woke up and found them, she would know that he had tried to poison her. Also, we know from Dorothy that the rubbish was too heavy to carry. Well, if it was too heavy for Dorothy, then it would have been too heavy for Agatha, given that she's weak anyway. And we know she's not the most fastidious person, after all.' Now I looked triumphant. The rubbish was the key for me. I had been pondering it all day.

Martin sighed. 'It's still speculation, Soph. I mean, to me, this fellow Anthony White, Tony or Sid, or whatever he's called, is the prime suspect, what with the life insurance policy and all – I can't believe I'm saying this. It's beginning to sound like *Double Indemnity*.'

'Well, that's what I would have said too, until I really thought about it. You see, Anthony is very meticulous with paperwork. That's his *raison d'être*, if you like. There is just no way he would kill Agatha for life insurance and make it look like suicide if there was a suicide clause in the policy. That's assuming that he would kill her anyway, which I doubt. I can't see he would have any other motive than money. He'd put up with her for thirty years after all. Why the big change now?'

Martin looked at me in exasperation. 'What can I tell you, Soph? It's a good story and you tell it well. Maybe Agatha was right. Maybe you should be a scriptwriter. But even if I said I believed you, no one else will.'

'Why not?' I bristled.

'Well, I mean, yours is one story. There could be thousands of others.'

'Like?'

'Oh, I don't know about Agatha, but just think, for

example, if someone, say, that old man over there –' He pointed at an old man who was drinking stout in the company of his dog. 'He's looking at us now, and what is he thinking? Well, he might think we are talking about a possible murder, but it's pretty unlikely, no? He might think that we are a married couple arguing in a bar. He might be thinking that you are a tart I've picked up and we're haggling over the price – That wasn't meant to sound insulting, Soph, I'm just hypothesizing. He might be thinking we are two old friends discussing politics. I don't know ... There's no proof beyond reasonable doubt, is there?'

'But what about reasonable conscience? Isn't that more important?' I cried.

'You mean, you can't stand it that if what you believe happens to be true, the murderer gets away with it.'

'Yes. I do mean that. Anyway I think Agatha was trying to tell me something. I mean, she rang.'

'Yes, but you couldn't understand what she was saying.'

'True, but she left that note. I think she was trying to say "Sophie Listen". Because on the tape she's talking about going to New York. She didn't want to die.'

'But that tape was recorded before she got the all-important mystery phone call, wasn't it? God, I can't believe I'm taking this seriously ... You've got to stop this latter-day Miss Marples stuff, Soph. I mean, as far as I can see, it won't make any difference. Nothing's going to make Agatha live again, is it? And we're hardly talking about a potential serial killer here, are we?'

'Well, he killed Chutney too!' I stammered, tears rolling down my cheeks. 'He might be a danger to Dorothy,' I added pathetically.

'It sounds to me like she is more of a danger to herself. And, anyway, don't you think she must know, subconsciously at least, if what you say is true? I mean, if he did go at all, Jack must have come home in quite a state. I shouldn't think he told her where he had been, but she must have suspected. Wives always know, you know. At least, that's how it looks on *Crimewatch*.'

That brought me up short. I thought about it for a few seconds, and it served only to confirm my ideas. So that was why she was in the flat that day, trying to eliminate clues. She was protecting her husband, because he was all she had left.

But it was beginning to dawn on me that Martin was right. Perhaps the saddest thing about Agatha's death was that no one except me really seemed to care very much what the truth was. There hadn't been much truth in her life, so maybe that was unavoidable. And however much I knew my theory to be true, I had no evidence, apart from little bits of a life history I had been privileged to glimpse, and my instinct that she just wouldn't have killed herself. I felt I knew Jack Burton from his work, knew how he would feel if he thought he could have been famous and had been stopped. But perhaps I was just romanticizing, as many women do, about angry young men.

I thought about that for a while, then looked up at Martin. He clearly thought that I had been so disturbed by Agatha's death that I was trying to impose my own kind of logic on it. By making it into a murder, I could understand it better, or transfer some of the guilt I felt on to someone else. It was a possibility that I had considered myself several times in the early hours of the morning. Martin's face was contorted with worry and concern. It touched me. I knew he was only trying to look after me. To save me from getting myself into more trouble.

I excused myself and went to the toilets. I spent a long time washing my hands and drying them under the automatic dryer. Somebody had scrawled next to it 'Now wipe your hands on your jeans.' I smiled at that, and looked at myself in the mirror. I was standing at another crossroads. I had to decide whether to keep delving into the past or step out into the future.

I walked back to our booth, put my arms around Martin's shoulders from behind and kissed the top of his head. He found my hands and held them in against his chest, and we rocked back and forward together for what seemed like a long time.

The old man across the bar drained his stout, put the empty glass down and saluted us silently as he left.

Then the bartender announced last orders. We both had empty glasses and were the only people left, so we decided to go. It was early yet, but the pier was closing. We started walking back holding hands, but then Martin saw a shooting star and pointed at it.

'You're meant to make a wish,' he said.

I clung to the balustrade, yearning to see it, but it had gone. I stared out over the churning pewter sea.

'Come on, Soph, we might still catch the eight-fifteen if we get a move on,' said Martin, striding out ahead.

In the train we chatted half-heartedly for a while about the latest political events, and about Martin's proposed skiing holiday at Christmas, then I said, trying to brighten us both up, 'So what's the latest on the air hostess?'

Martin blushed. 'I was hoping you wouldn't ask . . . You see, I'm having a bit of difficulty with it all.'

'Meaning?'

'Meaning that yes, we have . . . and it was very nice. It was a bit like bonking a fantasy woman . . . Do you know what I mean?'

'Like me and Laurence Harvey in *Room at the Top*.'

'Well . . . more like Kim Basinger in *Blind Date* for me.'

'Why not *Nine and a Half Weeks*?'

'Well, I didn't like her so much in that. She was too masochistic . . .'

'Martin, why are you such a lovely man?'

He looked embarrassed.

'The trouble is,' he continued, 'that there's nothing more than that. You know, I thought I really loved Darryl.'

I winced at the name.

'But I don't. She's a beautiful woman and she is extremely nice, but there's something missing.'

'Like what?' I said, leaning forward, intrigued.

'Oh, I don't know, like soul, or something. The other day in bed she was having a nightmare. It woke me up and I thought, rather unkindly, I suppose, that now . . . now, finally, I would see something of her inner life. She was thrashing about desperately in bed. I tried to calm her down and hear what she was talking about, and you know what it was?'

'No?'

'That there weren't enough Hand-i-Wipes to go round for courtesy drinks on the short hop between Lanzarote and Fuerteventura. The plane had been delayed, you see. That is what she dreams about.'

'So what's the problem?'

'Well, I think I'm going to have to move. I mean, ever since we first, you know . . . Well, I can't get rid of her now. And I can't hope to have a real relationship with her.'

I'm ashamed to say that I laughed.

'Well, don't say that I didn't tell you!'

He looked hurt, then countered, 'So, Sophie Fitt, what about your love life?'

'Nothing,' I said, disingenuously.

'So who was this "client" that you mentioned before? Don't think for a moment that you got away with that.'

So, between Preston Park and Hassocks (it was a stopping train), I told him about Greg.

'I don't know what it is about men and me,' I ended.

'I think it's because you think too much,' said Martin.

'How can you say that?' I cried.

'Well, of course, I love it ... that you do,' he said quickly, 'but in my experience, most men can't really deal with that. In Greg's case, that's not surprising, is it?'

'I suppose not,' I said. 'So what am I to do, stop thinking?'

Martin laughed and begged me not to.

'So what are you going to do now?' he asked, when he had contained himself.

I told him that I was seriously thinking of leaving the country for a while. I wanted to find my father and talk to him as an adult. Martin looked a bit perplexed at this. Maybe I would learn a new language, travel and then just see what came up, I said. After all, there didn't seem to be anything for me at the moment in England.

'But what about your act?'

'Martin, I know you're only trying to be encouraging, but £10 once a month for a stand-up routine in an Islington pub is hardly going to keep me, is it? Anyway, the last show was terrible. I know I'm on probation now and I haven't got an idea for the next one.'

'But you're good at it. Honestly, I think you're far better than some of the people on television.'

I thanked him, but said I thought he might be a bit biased.

'Well, you must be able to do something with all the material you've amassed in the last couple of months, surely?' he said.

I thought about it. A job as a temporary secretary, a boss who dies, a love affair that goes drastically wrong. There didn't seem to be many laughs in that. I changed the subject.

From Gatwick Airport to Victoria we played Botticelli. I think we both acknowledged that we didn't want to talk about anything further that evening. And sometimes I ask myself why I didn't see the shooting star on the pier, and why I didn't grab his hand and make a wish, and why we didn't just fall into a hotel in Brighton together that night?

My mother is right, Martin is the man I should marry. But I think that sometimes you like someone so much that you just don't dare step into uncharted territory, because it just might be dangerous and you might find things that you don't like, and if you're happy enough in someone's friendship, why gamble on paradise?

Martin disappeared down the tube. I waited in the taxi queue and tried to think positive thoughts under the dripping parapet of Victoria Station.

30

The inquest recorded a verdict of death by misadventure.
I suppose that meant that Anthony got his lump sum. I
wasn't called upon to attend. I imagine that Anthony
bought Dorothy out of her majority shareholding, because the next time I passed the entrance to the office
the Brown and Brown brass plaque had been taken
down and a less discreet one with a logo proclaiming
'Anthony White. Theatrical Agent 3rd Floor' had replaced it. I was on my way to the memorial service in St
Martin-in-the-Fields. It was rather a jolly affair, with the
actors and directors Agatha had represented lovingly
reciting her favourite bits of Shakespeare, and other
plays. For all her cynicism, I felt that she would have
been touched by the number of people there, and the
fact that they were genuinely moved by the service and
the readings. The church was filled with the scent of a
thousand flowers. I noticed that Dorothy – I could never
forget that black coat – was standing in the front row,
unaccompanied, and swaying a little.

Instead of a last hymn, the group of actors sang 'Sit
down you're rocking the boat' from *Guys and Dolls*. It
sounded odd with an organ accompaniment, but I felt
she would have liked it for that very reason.

I slipped out from my pew towards the back as soon as
the last note sounded. I felt a bit of an impostor and I
wanted to get away quickly, but it had snowed while we
were inside and I paused for a second as the cold air hit

me and marvelled at the dull gold vista of sparkling sun meeting frozen rain over Trafalgar Square.

I felt a tap on my shoulder. I turned round frostily, then smiled. Greg beckoned me away and we ended up in the American Bar of the Savoy, drinking proper Martinis and toasting Agatha in a way she would have approved of, for far too long.

I never did meet Jack Burton, although I suppose I shall come face to face with him in a few minutes' time.

Martin, who was in Los Angeles on business, tore out a piece on the 'Season of Seminal Works from the 1960s' from a magazine. *The Hairs in the Sink* got a one-line mention as an enigmatic piece which always avoided confronting reality.

Of course, I hadn't been able to resist going to see Mr Middlemarch and telling him my thoughts about the rubbish. He took patient notes and shook my hand courteously as I left, saying patronizingly that the police were always grateful for the vigilance of the general public. It must have embarrassed him no end to have to ring me many months later.

I had just returned from Edinburgh, where I had my own billing on the fringe with *Something Funny* – a one-woman show about a slightly paranoid person who sees conspiracy at every opportunity, and whose refrain is 'There's something funny going on here . . .' One afternoon I was passing the Assembly Rooms and noticed the heated reviews for Jack Burton's comeback play, *For Old Times' Sake* ('Angry young man still raging . . .', 'Kill to get tickets for this . . .'), and I engineered, by flirting outrageously with the box-office attendant, to get myself a seat for the matinée.

It was a two-hander. A middle-aged couple, who were

lovers in their youth, meet for the first time in years when he comes to visit her in a home. She has Alzheimer's disease. Their conversation is disjointed, incomprehensible at first. The audience started tittering with embarrassment, but gradually sense begins to emerge, because the writing is so very clever. The history of their love affair and their feud comes back in fragments between mouthfuls of the chocolates he has brought her.

The actress's performance was remarkable. On several occasions, when the rest of the audience were laughing out loud at her outrageousness, I was silently weeping at her authenticity. If you exaggerated Agatha by a degree, she became this poor woman. By the end of the play, virtually everyone was crying, because they didn't know what to think. One could feel sympathy for the lover who had given her the poisoned chocolates, and maybe it was a better, more humane death. But I think that most people agreed with me. They would have preferred to have her alive, however barmy, and they condemned the man who had decided, with whatever intent, to kill her.

I thought at the time that he must want, at some level, to be found out. But even I accept that a literary critique would not stand up in court.

From what I've been able to gather during the first two days of the trial, Dorothy finally turned him in. Apparently Jack had a very public affair with his leading lady and, well, Dorothy never was very good at keeping secrets.